Send Me An Angel

Also by

Chris Walters

The Tashaverse:
No One Like You
Make It Real
Send Me An Angel

Goddess Good

ISBN: 978-1-964292-09-0

eBook ISBN: 978-1-964292-08-3

Visit the link below to listen to the Send Me An Angel playlist on Spotify.

For everyone who has ever needed a second chance.
For everyone brave enough to look inside themselves and decide it's
time to grow.

Content Awareness

- Brief allusions to extremely poor parenting. (not depicted)

- Infidelity (alluded to by MC and depicted by a jackass non-MC)

- Explicit sex between consenting adults

- Pregnancy risk

Contents

1. Owner of a Lonely Heart — 1

2. Lean on Me — 7

3. Friends In Low Places — 10

4. Complicated — 22

5. Hungry For Heaven — 32

6. Wish You Were Here — 50

7. Opportunities (Let's Make Lots Of Money) — 56

8. Over The Edge — 61

9. Stray Cat Strut — 68

10. Kashmir — 76

11. Missing You — 79

12. Miss Mystery — 85

13. Gonna Make You Sweat (Everybody Dance Now) — 94

14. Would I Lie To You? — 101

15. Everywhere — 111

16. Edge of a Broken Heart   117

17. Teenage Dirtbag   122

18. Laid   129

19. Jessie's Girl   133

20. Tubthumping   137

21. Purple Rain   142

22. Flirtin' With Disaster   148

23. You Oughta Know   153

24. I Will Survive   159

25. Changes   164

26. Nobody's Fool   172

27. Pretending   179

28. Amour   186

29. Alone   192

30. Hold Me Now   201

31. Don't Stop Believin'   207

32. Blind Faith   215

33. Learning To Fly   221

34. Desire   228

35. I Want You To Want Me   234

36. Blow My Fuse   242

37. Slow Ride	249
38. Astronomy	256
39. You Shook Me All Night Long	260
40. High Enough	266
41. Afterword	271
Acknowledgements	274
About the author	276

Chapter 1

Owner of a Lonely Heart

Yes

Brad Kowalski was mentally and physically exhausted as he pulled his pickup into the driveway of his new house. The drive from Eastern Oregon to Seattle was arduous in the best of times, and early December was not ideal for navigating the Pacific Northwest weather. He made it safely with the trailer still attached and started unpacking immediately. Four hours of effort left him dusty and sweat-soaked. Looking around his new place solidified the reality of his situation.

Walking into a new home with Megan ten years ago held so much more promise. Then I screwed it all up. Megan has a new home, a new girlfriend, and a new life with our daughter. Here I am, alone in a brand new city, with takeout food, an air mattress, and a sleeping bag, hoping for a fresh start.

Brad woke up early Tuesday morning, shook off any lingering melancholy, and got going. He went grocery shopping and did as much as he could to make his new place more home-like. Brad looked forward to a furniture delivery from Ikea later in the week—he desperately wanted to sleep in a bed again. With the limited amount of stuff he brought, settling his few possessions didn't take long.

Now is as good a time as any to explore my new neighborhood. Maybe I'll grab lunch at the brewpub down the street and have last night's leftovers for dinner.

The pub was only a short walk, so Brad grabbed his coat and braved the cold Seattle drizzle. He took a seat at the bar and ordered what turned out to be an adequate fish and chips and an excellent lager. Brad spent the time searching Google Maps for things to do nearby. Seattle had quite a few museums, an outstanding public library, and a lot of parks. He was looking forward to doing outdoor activities when the weather improved. For now, though, Brad needed something indoors, and a yoga studio caught his eye.

Megan loved teaching yoga. She stood by its physical health benefits just as much as the mental balance it promoted. I really should have supported her more, especially when the rest of the town decided yoga was un-Christian. Just another thing to add to the long list of reasons she left me. I'm such an asshole. Yeah, mental balance sounds good right now.

The studio website showed a late afternoon intermediate class with a few openings. Brad booked a slot and spent the rest of the afternoon wandering through the neighborhood, leaving enough time to clean up and change before yoga. He arrived early, wearing sweatpants and a Kraken t-shirt. Brad filled out the forms and paid for his class, noticing the receptionist was eyeing him strangely.

Brad queried, "Is there something wrong?"

"Sorry, I'm just noticing you don't have a yoga mat."

"Oh, right. I just moved here, and mine got lost," Brad lied.

"Would you like to purchase one? We've got a fifteen percent off sale for the holidays."

"That's a good call. Let me pick one out." Brad grabbed a black yoga mat and paid for it.

Walking into the class, Brad suddenly felt very out of place. His sweatpants and hockey t-shirt contrasted vividly with the uniform yoga pants and crop tops everyone else wore. He shuffled to what he hoped was the back of the class and set down his mat and water bottle, trying to ignore the subtle stares. To get limbered up, he did some stretches he remembered from his days playing baseball.

The instructor turned on mellow Indian music and began leading the class through the opening exercises. She moved gracefully and spoke with a soft yet forceful tone. Brad couldn't understand half of the phrases she used. He did his best to imitate her complex and perplexing movements, but all too often, he staggered.

I feel like an elephant trying to dance ballet. I have no idea what the instructor is telling me to do. Holy shit, this hurts. It hurts a lot.

The woman to his right noticed his struggles and took pity on him. She toed her mat closer to his. "Watch what I do. I'll try to guide you through this," she whispered.

Brad whispered gratefully, "Thank you."

He focused on her as she continuously whispered guidance and hints. Brad did his best to mimic her movements as his muscles protested and sweat poured down his face.

"It's okay to stop if it's too much."

Pride fully engaged, and he shook his head in response.

Brad was trying to hold a stance called a warrior two when the instructor walked toward him. She gently touched his new partner's arm and whispered to her. The unknown woman smiled and nodded back. Then, to Brad's immense dismay, the instructor had everyone shift their stances, and the back of the class suddenly became the front. Brad felt like every eye was now focused on him. His clothes were sticky with sweat, and his muscles vibrated like the cables of a suspension bridge in a hurricane. He breathed a haggard sigh of relief when the focus of the class shifted back to the front. When the class ended fifteen minutes later, he collapsed on his mat.

Brad groped desperately for his water bottle, even though he knew it was empty, but he couldn't find it. His legs felt like Jello, and he didn't trust himself to stand. Head down and abjectly miserable, he felt a metallic tap on his shoulder. Brad looked up to see his water bottle in the hand of the woman who helped him.

"I filled it up for you."

"Oh my god, thank you. You are a lifesaver."

"A lifesaver?" She laughed gently. "I always wanted to be a hard, round candy that tasted vaguely like fruit."

"Oh...right. You're funny." Brad might have laughed if he had the energy, but he didn't.

"Let me guess, you've never done yoga before, but you decided you were an athlete and could go straight to intermediate." Her voice dripped with wry sarcasm.

"Was I"—Brad gasped—"so obvious?"

The woman laughed. "You're hilarious. My name is Devika. I'm usually at a beginner class on Wednesday night. Maybe you should try starting at the initial level first and work up to intermediate."

"Thank you. I'll do that." Brad paused to catch his breath. "Thank you so much for helping me out today. I'm serious. I don't think I could have made it otherwise."

"Like I said, you can always stop if it's too much. No one judges you if you need to take a break."

"Really? Because I felt judged today."

Devika arched an eyebrow at him. "*Dude*, you were a noob in an intermediate class. Everyone could see it. You aren't the first idiot, and you won't be the last."

Brad huffed, his heart rate slowly climbing downward. "You're saying that everyone is used to dumbass men trying this."

"Pretty much."

"I'm not sure if that makes me feel better or worse."

Devika reached out. "Need a hand up?"

Brad grasped her hand and tried to stand, nearly pulling her down when his legs buckled. Luckily, her grip was strong and she had phenomenal balance, allowing her to stay upright. She braced herself, and when Brad nodded, she pulled firmly until he was standing. Brad staggered, and her hands flew to his chest to gently nudge him back as their bodies almost touched.

"I'm sorry. I didn't mean to be inappropriate. My legs—"

"It's okay. You're in rough shape right now. Can you walk?"

"Maybe?" Brad shuffled one foot slowly forward.

"Stay there. Give me a minute and I'll help you."

Brad nodded weakly, swaying in place. Devika rolled up his yoga mat and tucked it under one arm, her own mat slung over her shoulder. She slid herself under one of his arms and wrinkled her nose. "Ready to go?" Brad's head wobbled in assent before he shuffled off, leaning on Devika.

When they got to the front door, she asked, "Where's your car?"

"Um, I walked. I'm about four blocks away. I can make it from here. Thank you."

"You sure?"

"Yeah. I'm good."

Devika handed Brad his yoga mat, and he walked off. Brad made it about ten steps before he stumbled, dropping his mat and hanging onto a street sign for dear life.

Chapter 2

Lean on Me

Bill Withers

Devika watched the stranger leaning against the sign pole and wondered about his chances of making it home. She was tempted to let him suffer the consequences of his poor decisions, but her heart wasn't in it. "Damn it," she muttered under her breath. Devika trotted over to him. "Come on, tough guy. Let's get you home." Once again, she tucked herself under his arm to provide support. "Whew. Take a bath when you get home, preferably with Epsom salts if you have any. It'll help with the sore muscles, and..."

"I smell really bad, don't I?"

"Awful. Not the worst smell I've ever encountered, but yeah. It's bad, dude."

The man paused. "I'm sorry, I've been very rude. My name is Brad. Nice to meet you, Devika. You are incredibly kind to put up with me and my body odor."

"I didn't feel right to leave you slumped on the pavement until your muscles decided to work again. Also, Mummy would tell me this is just a drop in the ocean of my vast karmic debt."

"Like your good deed for the day. That's what we called it in Boy Scouts."

"Oh, a Boy Scout. I'm guessing the Scouts don't have a yoga badge."

Brad convulsed. "Ouch, it hurts to laugh. Really, everything hurts. I'm an idiot."

"Good for you. Socrates said the only true wisdom is in knowing you know nothing. Admitting you are an idiot is progress."

"Why does progress hurt so much?"

Devika attempted an Austrian accent. "As the great philosopher Arnold Schwarzenegger said, 'There is no gain without pain.'"

Brad moaned, "Oh my god, stop being funny. I'm dying here."

"More words from the great philosopher: 'I'm the party pooper.'"

"How can you be so good, yet so evil at the same time?"

"My mother says I have a special talent."

"She's right."

Devika giggled. "Aw, I'll tell her that when I talk to her. She always likes to be proven right."

They stumbled on in silence, although Brad did get better as they went. Eventually, they came to a bungalow. Brad said, "This is me."

"All right. Let's get you inside."

Brad fumbled for his keys at the door and groaned when they fell to the ground.

"You're having challenges tonight. Just stand there, and I'll get the door for you."

Devika opened the door and helped Brad shuffle inside.

Wow, this looks like a serial killer's lair. Or at least a stalker. Devika didn't voice those thoughts, opting instead to ask neutrally, "Are you going for a minimalist vibe?"

Brad gave her an embarrassed shrug. "Sorry about the...everything. I just moved in yesterday, and there's furniture coming."

"Welcome to Seattle, then. Are you good to go from here?"

"Yes. Thank you so much, Devika."

"You're welcome, Brad. Have a good night." She gave him a little wave and closed the door behind her.

Now I need to get myself home and wash all of this man-sweat off of me. Note to self—don't pick up stray cats, stray dogs, or stray men. They all smell bad.

Back at her apartment, Devika threw her soiled clothes in the laundry and took her own advice about an Epsom salt bath. Feeling refreshed, she made *dal makhani* for dinner. Devika watched an eighties action movie while she ate. After dinner, she grabbed a couple of her favorite toys, and as the movie reached its climax, so did she.

Chapter 3

Friends In Low Places

Garth Brooks

The alarm woke Brad out of a sound sleep, and being awake felt like a nightmare. His muscles were stiff and sore in ways he'd never thought possible. Brad crawled laboriously off of his air mattress and painfully staggered to his feet. A hot shower helped ease some of the aching tension in his body.

What was I thinking? Oh yeah, I thought yoga would be easy. I'm never doing yoga again. I definitely shouldn't have done anything that stupid before my first day at a new job. Of course, if I do go to yoga again, I might see Devika. Seeing her seems like a good idea—al-

though, given my track record lately, perhaps not. She was incredibly kind, but maybe she thinks I'm an asshole. She is pretty, though. But my ex-wife was pretty, too, and look how things turned out. Right, because I'm an asshole. I hate myself.

Brad managed to get into his suit and eat breakfast. Getting into his truck was much harder than usual, his muscles protesting every movement. With a groan, he settled himself in and started driving. He traveled against the flow of rush hour traffic, so his commute wasn't long. Brad parked in front of the credit union and walked to the front door. The door was opened by an attractive woman who introduced herself as Melissa, from HR.

Stop thinking of your co-workers as attractive, Brad. Not keeping your hands off a co-worker is a large part of why you're divorced.

Melissa introduced the muscular young man with her as Jamari, from IT. Brad shook hands with both of them, wincing slightly at Jamari's grip.

"Hey, man. Sorry," Jamari said.

"Nah, it's totally cool. I tried yoga yesterday, and I'm paying for it today."

"Damn, man. Yoga is rough. I'd rather do deadlifts and squats all day than yoga."

"I'm with you."

Brad could see Melissa's eyes dancing with amusement at the two men before she asked, "Is that your truck?"

"Yeah. Is there a problem?"

She frowned. "Obviously your vehicle is your choice—as a community credit union in the Seattle area, we're looking to show community awareness and reduce our carbon footprint."

All right, Brad. Try very hard not to say anything stupid right now. You promised Megan you would be a better man. Someone Sophia would be proud to call her daddy. Also, you need this job, so don't piss off the nice HR person on your first day. Take a deep breath and respond thoughtfully.

"You make a fair point. Thank you, Melissa. In Eastern Oregon, a pickup truck is pretty much standard issue, but I'm here now. Do you have any suggestions?"

"Actually, yes. Seattle has an excellent public transit system, and Friday is the deadline to apply for the transit benefit for January. It's a pre-tax deduction from your paycheck and provides a monthly transit pass. You can defer a month if you happen to be traveling or have family issues. I'm happy to walk you through the process."

Don't be a macho douchecanoe, Brad. "I would appreciate your support."

Melissa's eyebrows betrayed her surprise, but her face settled back into professional mode. "Excellent. Jamari will get your hardware set up and take care of any tech needs. While he is working his IT magic, I'll go over your remaining paperwork—answer any questions you might have, especially around benefits. It might interest you to know that with our healthcare plan, joining a gym or other fitness studio and attending regularly can reduce your insurance costs. We also have a competitive wellness program with incentives, so regular exercise is financially beneficial as well."

"Awesome, let's get started. Does a fitness studio include yoga?"

"Wonderful. Yes, yoga is included." She quickly hid the hint of a smirk. "Now, since most people ask about healthcare, we offer employee-only, employee-plus-spouse, employee-plus-dependent, and family plans. Do you know which suits your needs?"

"Employee-only is fine. My daughter is on my ex-wife's plan."

The next hour was a blur of paperwork, password creation, and the other myriad minutiae of starting a new job. When they were done, Jamari handed him a new phone. "This is your work cell. I sent you an email with instructions on how to set out-of-office messages for your email and cell. If you have questions, then please contact IT."

Melissa chimed in, "We expect you to use your out-of-office messages. When you're not working, you should actually *not be working*."

"Do you mean not working, or are you just saying it because you're in HR?"

"We actually mean it. We live in a beautiful place, and we want everyone here to enjoy the city, nature, or both."

No wonder Dad hates this credit union with such passion. It is the antithesis of everything he is.

"Sounds amazing. Thank you both for your time."

After Melissa and Jamari left, Brad introduced himself to the staff as their new branch manager. He explained that he was new to the credit union and wanted to learn from them how they worked best. He spent time with each of them over the rest of the day, observing and asking questions. His goal was to build strong relationships with each team member.

If I ever get into a bind, I just need to think about what Dad would do in any particular situation and do the opposite. That should work at least ninety percent of the time.

The commute home was quick. Once there, Brad quickly grew bored. Cable and internet would be hooked up on Saturday, probably about when his furniture was supposed to be delivered. He could read, but he was feeling restless. Brad went out for a walk and soon found himself in front of the yoga studio.

This is stupid. I'm still sore from yesterday. Why would I even consider doing this again? Oh, right, because a pretty woman was nice and took pity on me, and she is taking classes here. Is there a worse reason to voluntarily sign up for torture? Probably, but I can't think of one. And yet, I'm opening the door and going to the counter. Because I'm a fool.

Brad bought a ten-pack of drop-in classes and a new pair of shorts. He considered yoga pants and then decided he would rather die than ever be seen in Lycra. As Brad finished paying, he felt a tap on his shoulder. He turned around to see brown eyes, like limpid pools of chocolate looking at him.

"Hey, stranger. I didn't think you would ever come back." Devika grinned at him below sweaty locks of raven-black hair.

"For your information, I just bought a ten-pack of classes. You might see a lot of me."

"Hmm," she sniffed. "Might not be so bad, especially since you aren't soaked in sweat."

Before Brad could respond, his stomach betrayed him with a loud rumble.

"Sorry about my stomach. I'm gonna go get dinner."

"No worries. See you around, Brad."

"Later, Devika."

Brad hurried home to drop off his purchases. From there, it was a quick walk to the pub. Walking in, he headed toward the bar when a woman's voice stopped him.

"Are you following me?" the mystery voice asked.

Looking to his right, he saw Devika sitting at a table with a man. "Oh, hi. Fancy meeting you here," Brad said lightly.

"Come join us," the man offered.

"Uh, sure." Brad walked over and was about to sit across from the man when he indicated Brad should sit across from Devika instead.

"Hi, I'm Manny, and you obviously know Devika."

"Good to meet you, I'm Brad."

"*Mr. Intermediate Yoga*. I've heard of you."

Devika slapped Manny on the arm.

"What? Was I not supposed to say anything?"

"I apologize for Manny."

"It's fine. I know it's a funny story. I'm sure if I ever stop hurting, then I'll laugh about it, too."

Manny pushed a menu toward him, and Brad perused the options while subtly observing the other two. They both had black hair and brown eyes. Manny's skin was lighter than Devika's chestnut brown, and she had more of an athletic build, while Manny was mostly skinny.

As Brad pushed his menu away, Manny asked, "So, what are you going to get?"

"Uh, I was thinking of a burger, but maybe I shouldn't."

Devika and Manny both laughed. He said, "I appreciate the thought. Neither of us are practicing Hindus, although let's not tell anyone our little secret because our parents *definitely* don't know."

"I see. Are you...?"

As in, is this guy your boyfriend, brother, or what?

Manny answered, "Devika is my best girlfriend." He grinned widely. "And my ex-wife." He earned another arm slap. "What? It's true."

"Sorry, I'm confused. Best girlfriend and also ex-wife?"

Devika sighed and put a hand on Manny's arm. "Our parents thought we were a good match, so we got married. It turns out our parents were very, *very* wrong."

Manny smirked, adding, "We had one very critical interest in common."

Confused, Brad asked, "Like what?"

"Hey, guys," said a voice behind Brad. Manny stood up to give a tall Black man a very passionate kiss.

Oh. I'm glad he's not dating Devika, but I'm not sure I'm comfortable now.

"Nelson, this is Brad. Brad, this is Nelson. As you might have surmised, Devika and I share a common interest in men."

"Pleased to meet you, Brad. I apologize for Manmeet. He's very exuberant."

"Manmeet?" Brad felt guilty about the suppressed humor in his voice.

"And now you understand why I go by Manny. Apparently, every American can't help but think of penises when they hear my name," Manny said in a long-suffering tone.

Devika chose this moment to chime in. "It actually suits you really well."

"Don't I know it," intoned Nelson with an infectious grin.

They all started laughing at the innuendo.

Well, we can all laugh about this. Talk to yourself, Brad. What's going on? I'm at a table with two gay guys. I don't think I've ever been this close to a homosexual, and I feel uncomfortable. Not true. My ex-wife is dating her college roommate, who is obviously a woman, and I had a lovely time sitting with them at roller derby. I'm trying my best to be okay with Megan and Tasha's love for each other. Logically, I should also feel the same about Manny and Nelson, then. Following along the logic train, it is in my best interest to hang out with Manny and Nelson, because if I can be comfortable around them, then I'll be closer to fully accepting Megan and Tasha's relationship. As Tasha has explained, repressing my feelings is bad. Acknowledging, confronting, and examining my feelings is good. I hate admitting Tasha is right, but she is—she's right.

Once the waitress took their orders, Manny spoke. "Not to put you on the spot, Brad, but, what do you do?"

"I'm a credit union branch manager."

"No, not what you do for work. What do you *do*?"

"Oh, um. Well, I just started yoga."

Devika snickered, then covered her face behind her glass.

Brad cleared his throat. "Clearly, I am still a beginner."

Nelson interrupted. "Wait, are you Mr. Intermediate Yoga?"

Brad glared at Devika, who hid further behind her glass. "Is there anyone in Seattle who doesn't know?"

"Maybe? I'm sure there are some tourists who don't know yet," she answered. Devika was doing a poor job of keeping the humor out of her voice.

Brad sighed deeply. "I also like skiing, camping, hiking, and kayaking."

"So, you're an outdoorsy type?" Manny asked.

"Yeah, you could say that."

"Brad used to be a Boy Scout," Devika interjected.

"Yes. I made it to Eagle."

"What about sports?" Nelson asked.

"He's a Kraken fan," Devika answered.

Brad chuckled, pleased she'd noticed. "Also true. I watch football and hockey. I'm looking forward to the start of the PWHL in January."

Nelson looked at him quizzically. "The what?"

"The Professional Women's Hockey League."

Devika put her glass down and leaned forward with a fascinated look on her face. "Hang on, you watch *women's* sports?"

Brad shrugged. "Truthfully, I just started this month, but yeah."

Her eyebrows arched. "Just this month? I *have* to hear this."

You can't hide your baggage forever, Brad. Might as well start now.

"I just moved to Seattle from Eastern Oregon after my divorce, which is final as of last week. My ex-wife and my daughter live in Portland. My daughter, who is eight, wants to start playing roller derby. This past Sunday, I was down in Portland, watching junior roller derby with her, my ex, and my ex's girlfriend. I'm going back to Portland in January to watch more roller derby. The adult home teams start playing mid-January, and I want to take Sophia to see them. And Megan and Tasha."

"Did your daughter play this Sunday?"

"Oh no. Sophia hasn't even tried out yet. Hopefully, next fall I can watch her skate with the Rose Petals."

"Oh my goodness," Devika squealed. "Rose Petals. That's adorable."

"You should see it. I still only have a vague idea of what's going on, but it's fun. The older kids, the Rose Buds, are incredible athletes. A lot of the younger ones are still learning, and they have limited contact rules because of their age. The teenagers, though—apparently some of the older ones have been skating competitively for ten years. It shows."

Devika said softly, "Wow, you're really passionate about this, aren't you?"

"Yeah. I guess I am. I'm going to every one of Sophia's games. Anyway, with my daughter playing roller derby soon, I started looking for other women's sports."

Nelson smiled. "All right. I've never watched hockey. You know, because there's no ice in Kenya. I do love cricket, though."

"I can't even begin to comprehend the rules of cricket."

"How about this, Brad? If you ever want to go to a Kraken game, or watch this PWHL, give me a call. You can explain hockey to me, and then I can explain cricket to you."

You're going to do this, Brad. For Sophia, and for yourself.

"What about Manny here?"

"Manny hates sports."

Brad scoffed. "That's just unnatural."

Nelson nodded vigorously in agreement "*I know.* I told him the exact same thing."

"Guys, I'm right here," Manny whined.

"All right, Nelson. It's a deal."

"Wonderful."

Manny changed the subject, asking, "Brad, I hear you are single." There was a loud thump underneath the table, and Devika's expression was suddenly pained. Manny chortled. "Hah. I cleverly hid my ankles behind my chair legs."

Devika mumbled unintelligibly.

"So, Brad. Single and looking to mingle?"

"Um. Definitely single. I wouldn't say I'm mingling, though. If the right woman were to come along, then that would be great, but I'm not actively looking right now."

"Huh. What might the right woman look like?"

Brad tried very hard not to glance at Devika, because clearly Manny was hinting her way. He paused before answering, "I feel like it's really about the right connection. Like I said, I'm not really looking."

Further inquiries were mercifully cut off by the arrival of food. Brad hoped he could avoid any additional embarrassing conversations.

Chapter 4
Complicated
Avril Lavigne

As much as she wanted to strangle Manny sometimes, Devika felt his heart was in the right place. He hunched his shoulders guiltily under her stare, avoiding her gaze as he tucked into his meal. A small sigh escaped her lips as she let her irritation fade and focused on her own food instead.

She knew Manny felt guilty about their divorce, despite her frequent reassurances that he shouldn't. Neither one of them wanted to marry the other, but they felt obligated to fulfill their parents' wishes, and they knew how beneficial the match was to Devika's family, as she was marrying up in caste. During the Partition, Devika's great-grandfather had renounced caste and taken the surname Kumar. Devika's parents both considered this a mistake and were obsessed with caste. Strangely, they never considered why a high-caste family would be so eager to marry off a son.

The first year of their marriage was awful. Devika and Manny argued constantly about the lack of sex and children. Eventually, Manny confessed that he was gay, which Devika then spent the next year trying unsuccessfully to cure. By the third year of their marriage, the two settled into a comfortable routine. Around the start of year four, Devika and Manny realized they loved each other in the way good friends do. Shortly after their fifth anniversary, Manny met Nelson. Devika noticed the change in his demeanor almost immediately and confronted him about the change. Once he admitted he'd found a man he loved, she filed for divorce immediately because she wanted him to be free to be with Nelson. Her parents were livid.

So, for the past three years, Manny has endeavored to repay my sacrifice by trying to find me a man. Unfortunately for me, Manny tends to consider any straight man with a pulse to be a potential suitor.

In the grand scheme of things, Brad is one of the better catches he's tried to land for me. Sure, he's recently divorced and a single father, which are two pretty huge red flags. Then there's the dumb, arrogant male trying yoga in an intermediate class thing, which is a third red flag. On the plus side, he's gainfully employed, presumably educated, and he did come back to yoga to try at the beginner level. Maybe yoga is more of an orange flag than a red one. He's around my age and fairly easy on the eyes, too. Ugh, he also said he's not looking for anyone right now, and I'm not going to pursue a guy who isn't interested.

Devika turned her focus back on the conversation just in time to hear Manny say, "Brad, did you know Devika works for the city government as a photographer?"

"No, but I'm intrigued. What does being a city photographer entail?"

She shrugged, trying not to make a big deal about her work. "I go where I'm assigned and take photos. One day, I might be shooting construction work for updates on progress, and the next, I'll photograph the mayor at a grand opening ceremony. A lot of what I do ends up on social media or in reports."

"Your job sounds fun. Busy, but fun."

"Mostly it is. The hours can be unpredictable sometimes."

"How so?" By the way, he was leaning in, Brad seemed genuinely interested in her work.

"The city does a lot of work at night, particularly construction and repairs. Then there are social events, like if the mayor attends a gala or sporting event. The Fourth of July is another one with speeches and fireworks. I also might be called on to document severe weather events."

"Wow. You do a lot. How are you not constantly busy?"

"Seattle is a big city, so I'm not the only photographer on staff. We try to break things up so no one is overloaded."

"At least you aren't working for morons then. How did you get into photography?"

The answer is a bit personal for someone I just met. There's just a lot of history I'm not going to talk about with a stranger.

"Photography was a hobby of mine growing up, so I'm making a career out of it. You know the saying about doing what you love, right? What about you? How did you end up in credit unioning? That *is* how you say it, right?"

Brad laughed. "Banking. Credit unions are basically banks that return profits to their members rather than shareholders. Um. It's a long story, but I guess I was always good with numbers and money."

He gave a vague answer. Sounds like he also isn't willing to go into details with a stranger.

Nelson saved her from trying to come up with a follow-up question by asking, "What influenced you to move to Seattle?"

Brad paused for a bit, taking a bite of his burger. "A lot of things. The easy answer is because I got a job here. I desperately needed a fresh start—somewhere away from Eastern Oregon. I didn't want to be too far away from Sophia."

"Why not Portland?"

"It's..." Brad looked really uncomfortable. "It's complicated."

Nelson gave Brad an apologetic look. "Sorry, man. I didn't mean to pry."

"No, it's okay."

"Look. I understand 'complicated.' My parents never accepted me for who I am. I'm their only son and they haven't spoken to me since I left for college in the U.S. twenty years ago. Two of my sisters talk to me, so I'm not totally without family. Thankfully, they both moved to the U.S. as well. I haven't been back to Kenya in two decades. Oh, plus I'm Black, gay, and an immigrant, which isn't an especially popular combination in this country in the best of times. Some days, I wonder if I shouldn't have moved somewhere else. At least in Seattle, I'm considered a person with rights and dignity."

Brad looked a bit guilty as he muttered, "Damn, dude. You've nailed being complicated."

My heart breaks for Nelson every time I hear him talk about his family. The mood is getting dark. Time for something lighter.

"Brad, tell us more about roller derby."

His head whipped from looking at Nelson to her. He smiled gratefully.

"Like I said, I'm still figuring stuff out. There's two teams, and they each send five skaters to an oval track. One skater is called the jammer, and they're the one who scores points. They get points by lapping their opponents. The other four skaters are blockers. If a jammer is tired, they can make someone else be the jammer, but I haven't quite figured out the whole process yet. Sophia could tell you all about it, though. She is so excited to play."

He looks so happy when he talks about Sophia. It's nice to see a father staying engaged in his kid's life, even when separated. I do wonder why he isn't in Portland, though. There's a deeper story there.

Nelson followed up, asking, "It's a banked track, right? Like in the movies?"

"No. The track is flat. I asked. Apparently, a flat track is easier to set up and maintain than a banked track. Cheaper, too."

"Makes sense."

"Another question," Devika said. "Do you know if there's roller derby in Seattle?"

"Actually, yes. There are multiple leagues in the greater Seattle and Tacoma area, including a few leagues with junior programs. There's even an annual juniors tournament early next year. I'm looking forward to the day when Sophia comes up here to play in that tournament. I'm sure she's going to be awesome."

"Speaking of, how does one become a skater? Is there a timeframe for all of this?"

"According to Sophia, she has to go to the boot camp next year. They'll give her an introduction to roller derby. Then, she would be placed in a training pool where she would learn the necessary skills to play safely. Things like how to skate, how to fall without hurting yourself, and how to use your gear properly. Once she understands the basic skills, and is physically capable, then she is eligible to be on a home team. They have a juniors home team season starting in September. If she wants to be on the travel team and is good enough, then she'll hopefully be chosen. Travel skaters can play teams from all over the country."

"Wow. Sounds pretty involved."

"Yeah, it is. Megan will have to handle most of the logistics. Um, she's my ex. I support Megan and Sophia in any way I can."

"That's why you're going to Portland in mid-January?"

"Right. Sophia is so excited about roller derby, and she's never seen the adult skaters before. Her excitement is infectious. Plus, it really is fun to watch."

"How are you getting there?"

"It's a month away, but I'm driving. Why?"

"Have you thought about taking the train? I've gone down to Portland a number of times, and I much prefer taking the train than driving. It's about three hours either way, but on the train, I can relax and read a book."

"Huh. I never thought of the train. I'll look into it. Thanks."

They returned to eating their meals in contented silence. Once done, Brad asked Manny and Nelson, "How did you two meet?"

They looked at each other before Nelson sighed and said, "Go on. I know how you love to tell this story."

Manny grinned. "Nelson is an architect, and we met at a real estate conference in Vegas. I'm an engineer for a construction company, which means it's my job to take the outlandish and often insane ideas people like Nelson come up with and turn them into reality." Nelson gave Manny a long-suffering look. Devika knew just how much they enjoyed teasing each other about their respective professions. "We ended up sitting next to each other on a gondola ride at Caesar's. I saw from his badge that he was also from Seattle, and we started talking. The next night, we went to watch the fountains at the Bellagio and we had the whole 'I'm gay, so am I' conversation during the show."

"Of course, Manny forgot to mention he was married to a woman. A stunningly beautiful and incredibly intelligent woman, I might add."

"Hush, Nelson. You already stole my husband, you can't steal my heart as well."

Nelson gave her a good-natured smile and a teasing eyebrow raise.

"Yes, yes. I will admit I was so smitten with Nelson that I regrettably failed to mention being married."

"Yes, the ever-so-minor detail of your loving and devoted wife," Devika added with a chuckle. Even back then, she hadn't been mad at him.

"Anyway, the incredibly honorable Nelson put a stop to our shenanigans once he learned about Devika, but we did go out a few times once we returned to Seattle. Nelson is correct to say that my ex-wife is as intelligent as she is beautiful, and she quickly figured out something was off. I should mention how incredibly caring and wonderful she is as well, because she almost immediately freed me from the bonds of matrimony so I could pursue Nelson unencumbered. Of course, she insisted on meeting him first."

"Damn right. I wasn't going to lose my husband to just anyone. Once I met Nelson and decided he was a good man, I happily set Manny free."

"Ugh, and she loves to remind me."

"I do not."

"Do too."

Nelson whispered *sotto voce* to Brad, "They do this all the time." Everyone had a good laugh.

"All right," Nelson said. "I think it's time for us to head out. We have a dog who needs to be walked. Brad, here's my card. I really would like to learn about hockey, if you're interested."

"Yeah, I'm looking forward to catching a game with you, Nelson. It was nice meeting you. You, too, Manny."

"Wonderful meeting you, Brad. Please, I'm begging you, go watch hockey with Nelson."

Nelson laughed. "He really does hate sports."

Devika added, "Bye, guys. Have a good night. Manny, I'll see you Friday, right?"

"Yes, see you then."

The two walked off, leaving Devika and Brad alone.

Well, this is awkward. Did they leave us alone together on purpose?

"Um, are you going to yoga tomorrow night?" Brad asked. Devika noted a slight flush in his cheeks.

"Yes, I'll be there. You?"

"Definitely. It's time to try out a more appropriate level. Speaking of, isn't a beginner class below your level?"

"Eh." Devika shrugged. "There are never enough truly intermediate classes. Plus, even in a beginner class, there are more challenging alternative variations, so I can still get a challenging workout."

"Good to know. Am I in for a world of hurt?"

"Possibly. Don't expect to do everything at first. Be mindful of your body. *Definitely* don't expect to get the poses right at first. If you want, I can set up next to you and help you out."

"That would be fantastic."

"Okay, I'm happy to support you. Lastly, just listen to your body. If something is beyond you right now, just accept what your body tells you. There's no shame in just doing a child's pose if you need to. The important part of yoga, like any exercise, is the conversation you have with your own body."

"Child's pose?" Brad looked puzzled.

"Don't worry. I'll teach you. It's super easy, and actually an amazing stretch, but very restful as well."

"All right. Um, thanks for letting me join you all tonight. It was much more fun than sitting alone at the bar."

"You're welcome. It was nice having the chance to get to know you, Brad."

"You, too. See you tomorrow at yoga."

"See you then. Have a good night."

"Goodnight, Devika."

Chapter 5
Hungry For Heaven
Dio

Brad walked home to his lonely house, thinking of the evening's events.

It's nice how I'm making new friends right off the bat. Lucky, too. Devika is very sweet, and it's kind of her to help me out at yoga tomorrow. Honestly, she has been nothing but nice to me, even without knowing me at all. Then there's Manny and Nelson. I feel more comfortable around them now, especially after getting a glimpse into Nelson's life.

What would I do if Sophia told me she was a lesbian? Just a month ago, I think I probably would have reacted how Nelson's parents did. Now...now, I really don't know. I'd handle it better than Nelson's parents have, for sure. I can't imagine cutting Sophia out of my life. Heck, if Sophia did turn out to be a lesbian, then I wouldn't have to meet her prom date with a shotgun in hand. Somehow, the shotgun joke was funnier before I had a daughter. What does that say about our culture if I might prefer that she was a lesbian than worry about some boy taking advantage of her? It doesn't say anything good about how we raise boys. Or about how I was raised, and how I treated Megan.

Fuck. Self-awareness is painful.

Speaking of pain, this house is awfully lonely. Maybe I should get a dog. At least I wouldn't be alone. I could get a cat, but I don't like cats. Brooding and standoff-ish. Dogs are more affectionate. I've always thought of myself as a dog person anyway. Then again, after roller derby, Sophia's next favorite subject is their cats. Their—that's a painful word. Sophia, Megan, and Tasha are a family, and I'm alone in a new city. I'll go to the shelter Saturday and see who is available to adopt.

Next item, what about Nelson? His offer seemed genuine. I seem to recall reading somewhere about how getting to know people with different experiences can help build bridges. His story is awful, and yet all too familiar. How many kids at my old church ran away because their parents didn't support them? Or were kicked out of their homes? Or the one boy I heard about a couple years ago who ate a bullet. Did he do it because his parents didn't accept him? Tasha was right—again—when she told me to pick a new flavor of Christianity.

There's another task. Find a new church where I'm not surrounded by assholes like my father. He was deacon of the church, and how many women besides mom did he screw? Oh god. He always wanted me to throw parties at home when I was in high school, even providing the beer. I thought he was the coolest dad ever, but maybe he just wanted teen girls over.

Brad shuddered. Just thinking of his father creeping on girls made him suddenly feel ill.

I'm glad I'm away from him. I feel like I'm only beginning to see what kind of monster he was. Moving to Seattle seems like a better choice already.

All right, back to Nelson. I'm going to go to a hockey game with him. I'll even learn about cricket. I don't think I'll ever understand cricket, but I'll try. He seems like a cool dude, and I haven't had someone to watch live sports with in ages.

With some decisions made, Brad took some pain meds and got ready for bed. He settled down on the air mattress, and sleep quickly caught up with him.

He woke up a bit early on Thursday to get ready for work and a walk to the bus stop. The walk wasn't far, and there were plenty of buses, so it wasn't crowded. He didn't have to transfer, and the walk from the other bus stop to the credit union was only about three minutes. He wanted to see how the return trip went in the afternoon, but he was leaning toward transit over driving for his daily commute. He put a message on one of the Slack channels, asking about spare Kraken tickets. Once the credit union opened, he worked with Julie, Miguel, and Yolanda, the other three employees, to better understand what they did.

I'm starting to see how much I've missed by letting Dad pull the strings. Immediately jumping into an executive role felt great at the time, but it stunted my knowledge of how things really work. I've learned so much from my co-workers over the past few days—not just about day-to-day operations, but about them as people. Dad is a fucking idiot.

There was a small rush at lunch and another in the late afternoon. Brad jumped into a teller's desk to help out during the rushes, something he never would have done before. Throughout the day, he received a few responses about tickets. He emailed Nelson, who instantly responded affirmatively. Brad snagged two tickets for next week. Overall, it was a smooth day, and he was pleased as he locked up.

After a painless commute home, Brad changed into his yoga gear and grabbed his mat. He was a few minutes early and was happy to see that Devika had already staked out a spot for them in a back corner of the class.

Brad greeted her, "Hi. Thank you for saving us a spot. How was your day?"

Devika smiled back. "My day was good. How about you?"

"Surprisingly great. I tried the bus today—which went well."

She flashed a grin and fluttered her hand at him. "Look at you, taking public transit."

"I know, right? Hey, are you sure you're okay with helping the noob out tonight?"

She gave him her warm smile again. "Totally. I checked in with Yvonne, the instructor. She knows I'll be helping you. What I want you to do is watch her and follow her lead. I'll be doing the same, but I'll jump in to help you if you get into trouble."

"Got it."

"You remember what I told you last night, right?"

"I think so."

"Communicate with your body and communicate with me. You got this."

"Thanks. I hope so."

Devika flashed Brad a broad grin. "I know so. One last thing. Do I have your consent to touch you?"

"Huh?"

"I need your consent to touch you."

"Sure, of course." Brad could feel his face coloring.

I feel like she just tested me, and I failed. It's not like I've never heard of consent before. Consent is just part of the basket of words and terms considered bad by the legions of people I once followed on the internet. Before Megan left me and Tasha delivered her ultimatum. From my asshole era.

She asked for my consent, and I just choked up. All those pro-grammed reactions screaming about how consent is 'woke,' or how anyone who asks for consent isn't a 'real man.' Because a 'real man' just takes what he wants, and that's supposedly the natural way of the world. What a real man I turned out to be. I took what I wanted and it destroyed my family.

Devika looked concerned. "Hey, are you okay?"

Shit. She can see something's wrong with me. I should go. I need to leave. I need to leave right fucking now.

Brad's vision was cloudy, and he felt his heart racing. Then, he felt it. A soft, warm hand on his arm. Firm fingertips on his skin.

"Brad, listen to my voice. I need you to take a deep breath for me. One, two, three, okay, you're doing great. Hold your breath, two, three, four. Slowly release your breath, two, three, four. Now hold again. One, two, three, four. Deep breath. One, two, three, four. Good. Hold for two, three, four. Release and do it again. Nod if you can hear me breathing."

Brad nodded.

"Good. I'm going to breathe in sync with you. Here we go, breathe in."

He felt his heart rate coming down, and the urge to flee dissipated. After a few cycles, he was ready to speak again. "I'm sorry. Thank you."

"No worries. Are you okay? You don't have to do this."

"It's...it's not you, and it's not yoga. I just have stuff going on. It's—"

"Complicated?"

"Yeah."

Brad looked at the instructor, Yvonne, who was staring at him with a concerned expression. Devika nodded to Yvonne, who nodded back and started class. The next hour was grueling. Brad did his best to follow Yvonne's instructions and motions. When he struggled too much, Devika was there——her firm hands guiding and supporting him, backing off if he grunted or when it was clear his body was bent as far as it could go. Throughout, she whispered soft words of encouragement.

Finally, Yvonne called them into *savasana*. Brad lay back quietly, following her instructions to feel how his body felt.

Like I've been wrung out to dry. I think I'm going to die. Actually, it wasn't completely awful. I managed to do some things. I made it to the end. Finishing is victory, right?

Once class was over, Devika checked in. "How do you feel?"

"Exhausted. Drained. Painful. Weirdly, kinda good." Brad chuckled. "Huh. Didn't expect to feel good. Yeah. I feel a sense of accomplishment."

"You're listening to your body. I'm really happy for you."

"I feel bad, though. You spent all class looking after me, which isn't fair to you."

"Don't feel bad. I enjoyed helping you discover yoga. I still got a good workout, and sometimes it's nice to not go all out."

Brad laughed. "All out was my only option."

"It gets better." Devika placed a hand on his arm again. "Like I said. Don't feel bad. I'm a grown woman who can make my own decisions."

"Got it."

"What's next for you?"

"Uh, probably back to the pub for dinner. You?"

"Brad, can I ask you something?"

Uh oh.

"Of course." He tried to make his voice sound more confident than he felt.

"Can you cook?"

"I can microwave stuff," he offered wanly.

Devika grimaced. "So...no. Let me guess, burger and fries at the pub?"

"Probably," Brad responded weakly.

Devika sighed deeply. "Come on. You're not eating at the pub tonight."

"Where am I eating?"

Is it wrong how much I hope her answer is, "My place?"

"It's a surprise. Do you need to change?"

"It would be nice."

"Fine, let's go back to your place so you can change."

Brad heard an edge of exasperation in her voice, but also something else he couldn't place.

At his door, Brad said, "Sorry about the place, I don't have furniture yet."

"It's fine."

He opened the door and ushered her inside.

"Um, let me get changed."

Devika frowned before asking, "Do you need the bathroom?"

"Sorry, I'm a poor host. There are two, so the guest bathroom is all yours."

"Thanks. See you in a few minutes."

Brad went to his room and changed into jeans and a flannel shirt. Once done, he returned to the main room.

What could be taking her so long? It's been at least ten minutes. Finally, here she comes. Oh...fuck...

Devika emerged from the guest room with her gym bag slung over her shoulder. Gone was the crop top and sneakers. She'd covered the yoga pants with a skirt, added a floral-print blouse, and finished the outfit with business-friendly yet sexy pumps.

"What?" she said. "Are you ready to go?"

Brad tried hard not to stare at her. "Yep. Let's go."

Devika set a hard and fast pace. Brad struggled to keep up—still a bit winded from an hour of yoga. His breath was ragged when she finally stopped. Before he could take stock of his surroundings, he felt himself being pulled through a doorway.

"Table for two, please," Devika said to the waitress, who led them to a cozy booth. She left menus and went to get them water. "Let me guess. You've never eaten Indian food before, have you?"

Brad felt an embarrassed flush in his cheeks. "Is it that obvious?"

She snorted. "Yeah. Like a gigantic, flashing neon sign. All right, Brad. What do you usually eat?"

"Burgers and fries. Steak and mashed potatoes. Fried chicken and tater tots."

"Oh, my god. You *do know* there are other vegetables besides potatoes, right?"

"Um."

"Is this what your ex-wife made for you?"

Brad sighed. "Honestly, Megan usually made something for me and then something else for her and Sophia."

"She had to cook two different meals because you're just a meat and potatoes guy?"

Wow. It really sounds awful to hear it like that. Devika sounds pissed, and she's absolutely right. I am such an asshole.

"I definitely want to find a clever way to spin this to make me sound like less of an asshole, but there truthfully isn't. To Megan's credit, she wanted me to try new things, but I didn't."

Brad could read the disapproval written across Devika's face as she asked, "Do you want to go somewhere else?"

"No. I made a lot of mistakes with Megan. *A lot.* She's better off without me, and honestly, she and Tasha are perfect for each other. I'm here now, and I'm trying to be better than the douchecanoe I've been all of my life. I don't want to leave, but I understand if you do."

Devika glared at him silently. The waitress came back with their waters and likely sensed the mood. "I'll give you two some more time to look over the menu." Devika's silent stare continued after the waitress scampered off.

Brad sighed in relief when she reached for a menu. He did the same, and he felt completely overwhelmed. His stomach nervously churned at the thought of so many exotic spices.

She already knows I'm an asshole. I might as well throw ignorance on top.

"What's good?"

Devika smirked at him. "Everything. Would you like suggestions, or would you like me to order for us?"

There was a time in my life when I never would have considered allowing a woman to order for me. And, honestly, that was just a few weeks ago. I need to be better.

"Order for us, please. I trust you."

Devika cocked her head, considering him intently. He could almost feel her mind working. His face flushed.

The waitress came back, and Devika asked a question in a language Brad didn't know. When the answer came in the same language, Devika then rattled off what Brad presumed was their order. The two conversed in this language for a few minutes, and then the waitress left.

"Um, I'm guessing we're good."

"Oh, we're good." Brad could hear a steely edge in her voice.

"Devika. I'm sorry I've upset you. You've been nothing but kind and welcoming to me when I've done nothing to deserve it. I was an ignorant dickhead when we first met, and you got me home safely. Tonight, you're doing your best to take care of me, and I still feel like a complete fuckwad. Thank you for your kindness. I'm sorry for putting you through this."

"You're definitely an ignorant asshole." Devika paused. Brad waited, hoping she had more to say. When she spoke, he released a breath he didn't even realize he had been holding. "You also clearly love your little girl. I feel like you are genuinely trying to make improvements, presumably for her if nothing else. Your effort and awareness counts for something."

"I made a promise to Megan and myself to become someone Sophia could be proud of. I haven't been that person for her whole life, but I'm making progress. I give Tasha, Megan's girlfriend, a lot of credit for not taking my bullshit, and really opening my eyes to just how bad I was. Tasha showed me what true love and support looks like. I'm so glad Megan found Tasha again. I can't change the past, but I'm happy for their future."

Devika's shoulders slumped, and her demeanor softened. "I get it. I made a lot of mistakes when I was married to Manny. Those first two years of our marriage—I was a total bitch. It wasn't entirely my fault. He could have been better, too. But a lot of it was me."

"I'm sorry. I shouldn't have said anything."

"No, it's good you did. I was feeling a lot of anger toward you. Not entirely undeserved." Devika paused and smiled. "But not entirely deserved, either. I had a great time with you, Manny, and Nelson at the pub. I saw the non-asshole side of you. Just something tonight flicked a switch, and I got worked up really fast."

"Thank you for talking with me. And thank you for saving me from another night of burgers and fries. Honestly, I'm not sure how I'm going to handle the spices. My stomach is tying itself in knots right now."

Devika laughed heartily while Brad chortled nervously.

"I won't lie—I strongly considered ordering you the *vindaloo*."

"Is *vindaloo* bad?"

"Oh no. *Vindaloo* is *amazing*. But it's also typically spiced to blistering heat. Indians are used to it because we grew up with it, but White boys like you—let's just say you would be in for a struggle for the next day or so."

"Food poisoning?"

Devika snickered. "No. It's when you discover that the second most mucus cells in the human body are around your sphincter. *Vindaloo* makes for an uncomfortable awakening."

Brad winced. "Oh. Thank you for not ordering me a dose of fire shits."

Her grin was wicked. "Don't thank me yet. Every good Indian cook learns how to vary spice levels. We serve fairly bland food to the very young and old, but the people our age typically like it spicy. We're quite skilled at ramping up the heat when we want."

"I see. Were you talking with the waitress about spice levels?"

"Yes. We had a lovely chat about you. You might have seen on the menu that there is a four-point scale ranging from mild at one up to Indian hot at four. What isn't mentioned is the zero spice level reserved for babies and the English."

"Why the English?" Brad saw Devika's cocked eyebrow. "Right, colonization. So what spice level are we getting?"

"Lucky for you, you said you trusted me, so we're getting mild."

"Thank you."

"And extra water. I suspect even level one might be interesting."

Brad tried to contain his anxiety. "Uh-oh."

"Don't worry. I'll be with you the whole time. Plus, I think you'll like this. I know how much you love your potatoes, so I ordered *saag aloo* for us."

"What's—"

"Hush, Brad. We're also getting *chana masala* and *dal makhani*. You need to learn about plant-based proteins."

"Like vegetarian?" Brad felt creeping disappointment.

"*Yes, vegetarian.* And because I am merciful, I ordered butter chicken."

"Thank you, oh merciful one." He watched a big grin spread across her face. "You ordered us a lot of food."

"I did.. We're both leaving tonight with a ton of leftovers. There's also rice and *naan*."

"What is *naan*?"

"Indian flatbread. You'll like it, I promise."

"Uh-huh." Brad was skeptical.

"You probably don't eat Mexican, either?"

"Nope. Why?"

"Mexicans and Indians use very different spices, but the artistry of the food is very similar. Lots of colors and dishes of varying complexity and spice levels." Devika leaned forward, her voice dropping to a conspiratorial whisper. "Don't tell my family, but I love homemade chili."

"Aren't you a vegetarian?"

"First, there are plenty of excellent vegetarian chilis out there. Second, I'm about ninety percent vegetarian. If I'm cheating, it's usually chicken or seafood, but"—once again she leaned in to whisper—"I've been known to have a burger, or even a hot dog."

Brad pulled back, his hand going to his mouth with a caricatured look of shock on his face. His voice mimicked false shock as he uttered, "Oh my, you wicked heathen."

They both giggled at their antics.

"I'm curious what language you were speaking."

"We were speaking Hindi. I'm fluent in Hindi and English."

"Is that the official language of India?"

"Good question, and a difficult one. Hindi and English are the only languages allowed in parliament, so kind of. India has hundreds of languages, and many states don't teach Hindi. Actually, Hindi is only used by around half of India. So, the first thing I asked our waitress was if she spoke Hindi."

"Hundreds of languages is kinda nuts."

"Is it? About a quarter of the United States was once part of Mexico. There are a lot of indigenous languages still in use. Hawaii was an independent country with its own distinct language and culture. Yes, English is the common language, but there are tons of others."

"I never thought about it that way."

Devika gave him a look clearly indicating he was being an ignorant asshole again.

"I see your look, and you're right. Thinking outside of my narrow worldview is one of those things I'm working on, and I appreciate you calling me out."

If Devika ever meets Tasha, then I'm going to be in deep trouble.

Brad was saved from making any further stupid comments by the arrival of dinner.

"Wow. Um, what am I looking at?"

"Let's make this fast. Hand me your plate. Thanks."

Brad watched as Devika spooned long, thin rice onto his plate.

"This is basmati rice. Here's some *naan*." She added a triangle of flatbread to the plate, then dipped a spoon into something dark and green. "This is *saag aloo*. The chunks are potatoes, the greens are—just try it. This dark dish is the *dal makhani*. Finally, these golden chickpeas are the *chana masala*."

"Didn't you mention chicken?"

"It's right here, but you have to try these first."

Brad fought to contain his disappointment. "Okay."

He took a forkful of rice and *saag aloo*, staring at it dubiously. There was an unseemly amount of green. Brad tentatively moved the fork into his mouth and took a bite. It was good. Mild and creamy greens, tender potato, and soft-but-firm rice all combined to please his tongue.

"Oh, man...it's so good."

Brad quickly tried the *dal makhani* and *chana masala*, enjoying those as well.

"Okay, Brad. Tell me what you think."

"I never knew—I guess I always assumed spicy meant hot. This is flavorful. Possibly a bit much, so thank you for making sure we had extra water."

"Come on, Brad. Surely you can do better than calling Indian dishes 'flavorful.' Food isn't just sustenance, it's personal—we express ourselves through what we cook and eat. We connect with others over food. I'm going to ask you again, tell me what you think?"

Brad contemplated his next words carefully as he ate—savoring the unfamiliar smells, flavors, and textures of each bite. Eventually, he crafted a response, "The spices dance on my tongue, working together in a harmonious blend."

"Awesome. A *much* better answer." She leaned forward, her eyes blazing with intensity. "Tell me something else. How do you *feel?*"

"I feel incredible. Electric. Like my life is somehow better."

Devika's smile was dazzling. "That's how food should be."

"I need to admit something. I've been exposed to food like this before. I met Megan and Tasha in college at Clemson. Tasha is from South Carolina, and she had us over to her family's place for a barbecue. I messed it up. All these preconceptions—no, that's not the right word. All these *prejudices* blinded me. I didn't want to eat anything. I didn't want to enjoy anything. I was angry I had to be there because I was dating Megan and Tasha was her roommate. I feel like I've missed out on so much because I was just stupid."

Devika looked concerned, and her voice was soft, but confident. "What's different now?"

"I fucked up and ruined my life."

"Right. And then what?"

"Now I'm trying to make a fresh start."

"Good. What can you do about the past?"

"Nothing, really."

Devika's eyes narrowed. "Come on, Brad. What can you do about the past?"

"I can't change it, but I can learn from it."

"And what are you doing now?"

He grinned once he made the connection. "Learning."

"You know what progress means, right? It's time for a reward."

Brad watched as Devika carefully moved a bowl full of an orangish liquid and chunks of what appeared to be meat toward him.

"What's this?"

"Chicken *makhani*. Also known as butter chicken."

Brad spooned some onto his rice and took a bite.

"Oh, my god. Now I know what heaven tastes like."

Chapter 6
Wish You Were Here
Pink Floyd

Brad got home loaded with leftovers, which went into the fridge. The food would last him for at least a day. He kicked off his shoes and dropped into the comfortable recliner. He hadn't brought much from the old house, but he couldn't bear to part with that chair.

Leaning back, he pulled out his phone and hesitated. Expelling a deep breath, he dialed a long-familiar number. He listened to it ring, expecting it to go to voicemail, but at the last second, the call was answered.

"What do you want, Brad?" Megan asked. She sounded exasperated.

"Hi, Megan. Is this an okay time?"

"Yeah. Probably."

"I want to say thank you to you, and also to Tasha."

"Wow. Not what I was expecting."

He continued softly, "I was terrible to you for a long time, and you never deserved any of what I did. And yet, even in the end, you were better to me than you should have been. I appreciate you."

"Uh-huh."

"You and Tasha have both been willing to give me the kick in the ass I needed. Tasha, I'm sure with more than a hint of glee." Brad chuckled wryly. "I've had a lot to think about."

"Brad, are you okay? Do I need to call someone to check on you?"

Another wry chuckle. "No, you don't need to. Thank you for checking, though. Am I okay?" Brad sighed heavily. "No, not really. I feel lonely, Megan. Before you say anything—yes, the loneliness is entirely my fault. I'm lonely, but there's hope."

"How so?"

"I just had my second yoga class tonight."

Megan cackled. "Hold the damn phone. Did I just hear that *Brad Kowalski* went to *yoga*?"

He laughed at her reaction. "Would it surprise you if I told you I tried an intermediate class the first time?"

"No. No, it doesn't. How much did you hurt afterward?"

"So much. It was so stupid."

He could almost hear tears of laughter in her voice. "Intermediate is a serious workout for me, and I've been doing yoga since college. What about tonight's class?"

"I learned my lesson and took a beginner class instead. I had some help, too."

"From the instructor?"

"Well, yes. But from another student who took pity on me after the intermediate debacle."

"*Oh, really?*"

"She helped me a lot. Last night, I ran into her, her ex-husband, and the ex-husband's boyfriend, and I ended up having a burger with them. I'm going to a hockey game in a week with Nelson, the ex-husband's boyfriend."

Megan's voice developed a sharp edge. "Brad. Why are you telling me all this?"

"I dunno. Partially because I'm lonely. Partially because I have some hope I might actually turn my life around. And partially because you and Sophia are the only family I can talk to."

"Brad..."

"It's not like that. I mean, I still love you, even after hopelessly screwing everything up. But you're with Tasha, and the two of you are perfect for each other. I just hope one day I can find a love as true as what you two share."

"What about your yoga buddy?" He could practically hear the arch in her eyebrow.

"Devika is super nice, but I'm pretty sure she thinks I'm an asshole. She's not wrong."

"On to other topics. How is Seattle?"

"Seattle is great so far. Thank you for resisting the urge to agree with me about being an asshole. You have plenty of reasons, and it's okay if you agree."

"Whew, thanks. Goddess, you are a fucking asshole. I'm glad you have hope of changing, though. Nothing would make me happier."

"Nothing? Really?"

"Fine. I'm not entirely sure I should tell you, but here goes. I proposed to Tasha."

"Wait. Proposed, like a marriage proposal?"

"Yes, marriage."

Strange. I would have thought her news would hurt more.

"She said yes, right?"

"She did," Megan purred happily.

"That's awesome. I'm very happy for you, Megan. For both of you."

"You really mean it, don't you?" She sounded surprised.

"I do. You deserve to be happy, and like I said, the two of you are perfect together."

"Thank you."

"You're welcome. Are you doing a big ceremony or anything?"

"No. I already did the big wedding with you, and Tasha doesn't want one of her own. She wants a small, intimate ceremony with close friends and family, which sounds perfect to me."

"We should have done the small thing." Brad chuckled. "Sorry, not like it matters. I shouldn't have even brought it up. Anyway, I wish you both the best."

"Brad? Do you want to say hi to Sophia?"

"I would love to, but first, can I ask you something?"

"Yeah, what's up?"

"The Rose City Rollers adult home team opener is in mid-January. I know it would be a late night for Sophia, but would you be okay if I took her to the game or if the four of us went?"

"You're going all-in on this, aren't you?"

"If it's important to Sophia, then it's important to me."

"All right. Let me think about it, and I'll text you with an answer."

"Thanks, Megan."

"Anything else?"

"Nope."

"Hang on." Brad heard Megan move the phone. "Sophia, come talk to Daddy for a minute."

Brad waited patiently until he heard a rustling on the other end.

"Hi, Daddy!"

"Hi, sweetheart. How are you?"

"I'm good. I was just reading with Nocturne and Julius."

"I'm sure they're nice cats. They seem to like you a lot."

"They do! They take lots of naps with me."

"How's school going? Are you making friends?"

"I am. The kids are nice. I've been eating lunch with Ruby a lot!"

"She's in your class?"

"Her desk is next to mine. She has a cat named Dolly Purrton."

"That's a funny name. I wanted to say it was good to see you on Sunday, and I hope to see you again soon."

"Me too!"

"I love you very much, Sophia."

"I love you too, Daddy!"

"Goodnight, sweetheart."

"Night-night! Mommy, here's your phone!"

"Brad?" Megan returned.

"Yeah."

"Thanks for calling. We're wishing you the best."

"Thanks for picking up, Megan."

"You're welcome."

"Have a good night."

"You too."

Chapter 7

Opportunities (Let's Make Lots Of Money)

Pet Shop Boys

B ack in her own apartment, Devika dropped her gym bag and leaned back against her door, clutching her leftovers. She went through her breathing exercises. For some reason, being around Brad made her feel off, but she couldn't understand why. Depositing her leftovers in the fridge, she walked into the main room, stripping off her skirt. She awkwardly yanked her shoes off and sat down in a lotus position. Devika called out to her Google Home system, instructing it to play meditative music.

She submerged into her meditation, slowly peeling away layers of anxiety. Years of practice helped Devika find her center and keep it. Enveloped in tranquility, she truly relaxed. Devika held onto her peaceful feeling for a while, until an urgent need to pee intruded. She surfaced, feeling the world rush back in. Now she was ready to handle it.

Tomorrow promised to be a long day, and she didn't need distractions. Devika stood up and got herself ready for bed.

The alarm went off unconscionably early. With a groan, Devika rolled out of bed to start the day. She had a pre-dawn photo shoot by the ferry, and she didn't want to be late. The Friday before Christmas was often a crazy day, but a favorite.

By noon, she was inside the Seattle Public Library, snapping photos of tourists and the city outside, using the magnificent architecture of the library itself to frame her shots.

Starting early meant leaving early, and today, she needed the time. Devika was meeting Manny for an Asian-American Real Estate gala and needed to dress to impress. She already had a *sari* picked out, but her outfit was less than half the battle. Manny picked her up in a company car, whistling as she approached.

"Shush. We both know all of this"—Devika gestured to herself—"is wasted on you."

"Just because you don't give me a boner doesn't mean I can't admire how stunningly beautiful you are, especially in your *sari*. You are the reincarnation of Maharani Tarabai herself."

"Flattery will get you nowhere." Devika paused and smiled. "But a girl does like to hear it anyway. Speaking of, you look very nice."

"Thank you, my dear. I dusted off my best Nehru jacket for this."

"You didn't dust it well enough." Devika sighed. "Come here." She leaned over and tugged at his jacket. "That's the best I can do in the car. I'll get you situated once we get out."

"Devika, darling. What would I do without you?"

"I don't know. Have Nelson dress you?"

"Hm, he does have impeccable taste, but, fortunately, he much prefers to undress me."

Devika rolled her eyes. "Too much information, Manny."

"Please. You know all of our dirty secrets."

"Ugh, I hope not." She got serious. "I assume most of your clients still don't know we're divorced?"

"Unfortunately, no."

"Manny, someone has to tell them sometime that we're not married, and that you're gay."

He sighed heavily. "I know. The firm's partners think it will hurt business."

"You're just catering to stupid homophobia. You know that, right?"

"It might be awful, but it's the truth. We're working with a Texas billionaire who switched to our firm because our competitor assigned him a lesbian project manager."

She rolled her eyes. "Hang on, was he pissed she's gay or because she wouldn't sleep with him?"

"Probably both. He's a douchebag."

Devika looked over at Manny in the driver's seat. "Speaking of your firm, don't your company cars usually have drivers?"

"Antonio is sick, and everyone else is already celebrating. I don't mind driving."

She nodded. "It's not like we were going to shag in the backseat anyway."

"Truth."

They spent the rest of the drive in silence. At the gala, the valet traded the car for a ticket. Devika and Manny linked arms and walked inside, smiling all the way. She hated the deception with a passion, but Manny was her friend, and she wanted to help him out. They cruised the crowd, mingling and chatting.

I enjoy these events, even if my 'marriage' to Manny is a tawdry masquerade. How often do I have the opportunity to dress up like this? So many new people to meet—at least some of them are interesting. The food is always hit-or-miss, especially the desserts. How hard is it to put out some simple chocolate items?

Devika's calves were getting sore by the time they made their exit. Climbing in the car, she propped her feet on the dash and gently massaged her muscles. She sighed as she gave herself relief.

"Another successful night, faux husband of mine?"

Manny giggled. "I see what you did there. Yes. Very successful. How are your feet?"

"Ugh. It's been a long day."

"You should have someone rub them."

Devika cocked an eyebrow his way. "Are you offering?"

"Perish the thought. My feet are hurting as well, and Nelson's waiting for me. Alone. In bed. If I'm lucky, naked."

She stuck her fingers in her ears. "La la la la. I don't need to hear any more."

"Sorry. I was just thinking...maybe you should call your new friend to"—Manny flashed her a lewd look—"relieve your aching muscles. Maybe even scratch your itches."

"Damn it, Manny. I appreciate you trying to set me up, but I'm fine on my own. Thank you very much. Plus, rechargeable silicone never disappoints."

"I'm sorry, Devika. I know your toys get you where you need to be, sexually, but I just want you to find love. I got lucky with Nelson, and I want the same for you."

"You want me to have Nelson?" Devika said devilishly.

"Stop. You know what I mean. Quit deflecting with humor."

"I know. It's so sweet you care for me like you do. Just, maybe try a bit less."

"Fine. Let's make a deal, Devika. I promise to stop pushing every single and straight male in Seattle your way if you promise to open yourself up to the possibility of love."

"That's a stupid deal."

"But will you say yes?"

"Ugh. Fine. I'll open myself to love. Whatever that means."

Devika didn't even have to look at Manny to know he was grinning ear-to-ear.

Chapter 8
Over The Edge
LA Guns

Brad had an early morning yoga class on Saturday. The timing was perfect as he would be home in time for the Ikea furniture delivery and the internet hookup.

Early morning is so different from afternoon. I haven't been moving, so this gets my blood pumping. My muscles feel tighter but loosen nicely as I go through the poses. I can see why Megan loves doing this. And Devika. I miss her presence. I know I'm being selfish, but it's true. Last night was my first class without her. I didn't think I would make it, but I did. Finishing on my own is a victory in and of itself. Still—it feels like there's an empty space when Devika isn't there.

Whatever. I just got out of a relationship. I don't need a rebound. Plus, she's probably happy she doesn't have to babysit a noob. And an asshole. Who knows, maybe I won't see her again and I'm just mooning over a stranger.

Brad tried to concentrate on relaxing through *savasana* but found it difficult to not think about Devika.

Stop it. Stop thinking about her. We're just strangers, briefly connected, now moving on.

The instructor brought the class to an end. Brad gathered his things and thanked her. He stopped at the desk, checking his phone for any messages. He felt gentle fingertips on his arm. Looking up, he saw Devika's smiling face.

Brad returned her smile. "Good morning, Devika."

"Hi, Brad. How was your class?"

"Good. I survived." He laughed self-effacingly.

"And without me. I'm not sure if I should be offended or proud." Her eyes danced with unvoiced laughter.

"I was in class last night, too. I miss going to class with you."

Shit. That was forward of me.

Before Devika could respond, Brad added, "You're my yoga buddy."

Whatever she had been going to say was discarded as she snorted, "Yoga buddy?"

"That's a thing, right?" The hopeful tone in his voice wasn't entirely joking.

"Maybe it is. I have an intermediate class in a couple of minutes—give me your phone."

Brad handed his phone to Devika. He watched as she sent a text, then pulled her phone out and responded. His phone dinged.

"There, now you have my number."

"Thanks." His mouth hung open, his brain unable to summon additional words.

"Maybe we can do a class together tomorrow. If you're up for it."

"That would be great, yoga buddy."

Devika giggled. "Text me—yoga buddy." She gave him a little wave and walked to class.

Brad shook his head and strolled home.

Yoga buddy—that was a good save. Thank you, Megan, for planting the seed in my head. I've been lonely since Megan left. Brad heaved his shoulders and sighed. *If I can't be honest with myself, then who can I be honest with? I was lonely long before Megan left. I'd shut myself off from her and Sophia. Burying myself in work to please my father, who could never be pleased. Then the affair with Margaret—we ended two marriages, and for what? Maybe if I had been a better father, husband, and person in the first place, then I wouldn't have cheated.*

These next few days will be brutal—Christmas Eve and Christmas, alone. Should I call Sophia on Christmas? Would it be better if she called me? What if she doesn't want to talk to me? Damn it. I can't think so negatively. I'll text Megan about talking to Sophia on Christmas.

Brad's melancholy was interrupted by the arrival of the internet installer. Before he was finished, the Ikea delivery arrived. Once he was alone again, Brad turned on some music to assemble the furniture. His top priority was the bedroom, so he started puzzling over the illustrated instructions for the bed.

Ugh. This is killing me.

Brad stood up and padded into the main room. Picking up the quick-start guide, he followed the instructions for setting up the wireless and connecting to the internet. It took him a few seconds to find instructional videos on how to set up his bed. Selecting one, he returned to the bedroom and got to work.

After he finished, Brad stood over his new bed, beaming with pride. Sure, he felt sweaty and gross, but he realized this was more than just putting a bed together.

I struggled with this project. In the past, I would have bulled ahead, hoping for the best. Instead, I stepped back, sought assistance, and then listened and followed the guidance. Now my task is done, and I know it's done right. I feel like I've made some personal growth.

Next task is the table, because I'm hungry. I'll eat some leftovers for lunch, assemble some more furniture, shower, and finally go to the shelter.

Brad arrived at the shelter later than he wanted, but with enough time to look around. He started with dogs. A gorgeous husky-mix caught his eye. Checking in with the volunteer, he learned there was already a hold on her, and a lengthy wait list. None of the few remaining dogs really connected with Brad, so he reluctantly moved into the cat area.

Brad meandered through, looking at the cats but unsure what to look for. He found a volunteer and asked her for help.

"What can I help you with?"

"I'm looking for a cat, but I have no idea what I'm looking for."

"Okay. Let's start with some basics. Have you ever lived with a cat before?"

"No, I haven't."

"What made you decide to get a cat?"

"Honestly, I would prefer a dog, but my daughter and ex-wife have two cats. Sophia loves those cats. It might be nice to have a cat if she comes to visit me."

"I see. What are you looking for from an animal companion?"

"It's hard to say. I'm kinda lonely right now—someone to share the space with would be nice."

"Huh, not much to go on. Are you willing to meet a cat?"

"Sure."

"Follow me into this room and have a seat. I'll be right back with someone I want you to meet."

Brad sat on a bench in a tiny room. There were cat toys strewn around, with more in a small box on the floor. He lifted his head as the volunteer returned, cradling a cat in her arms.

"This is Cricket." She gently placed the cat on the ground.

"Hi, Cricket. My name is Brad."

The small cat looked nervously around the room before scuttling under the bench.

"She's a bit shy."

"How did she get her name?"

"We don't know her original name. She was abandoned when her family moved away and left her. A real estate agent found her in the basement, where she survived by eating crickets. She's still a bit underweight, but she's improving. Cricket just came back from foster care."

"Wow, that's awful." Brad felt a nudge on his calf and looked down to see Cricket headbutting him. She slowly walked out from under the bench, rubbing against his legs. "Can I pick her up?"

"Let's see how she does with socializing first. Maybe try one of these toys."

Brad selected a pole and string with a feathered attachment. He waggled it in front of Cricket, who flitted behind his legs. She peered out, hunkering down. Brad could see her butt start to wiggle before she pounced. He pulled the toy up like a fishing rod, causing Cricket to miss. She landed, quickly resetting herself and leaping again. They went on like this for a few minutes. Sometimes, Brad would pull away in time, and others, Cricket would snare her prey. He could feel the smile blooming on his face.

Eventually, Cricket started to tire, so Brad put down the toy. He was surprised when Cricket hopped onto the bench and lay beside him. Brad gently stroked her soft fur. "I love her markings. She's so soft."

"Cricket is a tuxedo."

"Tuxedo? Right...she's mostly black except for the white patch on her chest. And another little patch under her chin."

"What do you think?"

"I think I'm smitten. Can I take her home?"

"It's too late to finish the process today, but I can put a hold on her. Tonight you have a chance to think about this, too. If you change your mind, just tell us. We're open tomorrow with limited hours, and we're closed on Christmas. We'll be back on Tuesday, though."

"Let's do the hold."

"Wonderful. Come on, Ms. Cricket. Let's get you back to your room, and then I'll help your friend with his hold. You might have a new human soon."

She was gently cooing to Cricket as she left. Brad stood and waited outside the little meeting room until the volunteer returned. He finished the hold process and went home.

At home, Brad looked on the Internet for advice about getting a cat. As he finished the leftovers, he compiled a list of items to purchase—from litter boxes to food to toys. He also checked the class schedule for Sunday and texted Devika. Then he texted Megan about Christmas and Sophia.

I'm excited about Cricket. She gets me, and I get her. We're two lonely souls in need of a friend and companion.

Chapter 9
Stray Cat Strut
Stray Cats

Brad woke up on Sunday with a smile. He ate breakfast and got ready for yoga, arriving at the studio a few minutes early. Brad spread his mat on the floor and started taking off his shoes when he heard a woman say, "Good morning, yoga buddy."

Looking up and over his shoulder, he saw Devika standing over him. "Good morning to you, yoga buddy."

They both giggled. As she unfurled her mat, Devika said, "This whole yoga buddy thing really is stupid, but it's cute, and I like it."

"Me too. I'm glad you like it," he whispered as class was about to start.

Later, as he lay in *savasana*, Brad's thoughts wandered back to the current class.

I made it through the whole class without Devika needing to help me. She looked like she thought about it a few times, but she let me continue. I'm proud of myself for improving. And I'm happy to have my yoga buddy back.

Slowly standing up after class, Brad asked Devika, "What are you up to for the rest of the day?"

"Nothing much. Reading and cooking. You?"

"I need to go shopping this morning, and later adopt my new cat."

Devika squealed. "You're getting a cat?"

"Yeah, I met her yesterday and can already tell we're soulmates."

"Is she as adorable as I want her to be?"

He chuckled. "Yes. Definitely. Do you have any pets?"

She shook her head ruefully. "I've thought about it, but life always got in the way."

"Too bad."

"Do you mind if I join you?"

Not an offer I expected. "I'd like to have some company. I gotta change first if you don't mind."

"Should I come with you?"

"You're welcome to, if you're comfortable."

"Sure," Devika affirmed before they walked over to Brad's place. Looking around inside, she commented, "Oh, you have furniture now. Nice."

"Sorry about the massive pile of Ikea boxes. I have to wait a few days before I can take it all to the dump. I also wasn't expecting company."

"Not a problem. I'm just glad your place looks less like a serial killer's lair."

Uh-oh. Do I give off a serial killer vibe?

"Thanks?" he ventured warily.

"Sorry, I probably shouldn't have said anything. I don't think *you're* a serial killer."

"Whew. Glad to hear it. Also, please ignore the fresh piles of dirt out back." Brad grinned.

"Nice. Joker." Devika shook her head. "Go get changed."

"Be right back."

Brad changed into jeans and a flannel shirt. He quickly checked his hair and brushed his teeth. Walking into the main room, he spied Devika on the couch in a lotus pose. Her eyes were closed, and she appeared to be breathing deeply.

And each breath is making her crop top do magical things. Stop. Be better, Brad.

"I can hear you. Are you staring at my tits?"

Yes.

"No?" Brad offered weakly.

Devika sighed. "Have you ever meditated?"

"No. My former pastor said meditation was a sure-fire path to hell."

"Ugh. Please tell me you don't believe his horseshit."

"I admit I used to. These days...let's just say that I'm reevaluating a lot of things."

Brad could see her cock an eyebrow at his admission. Her eyes were still closed, and she was keeping pace with her breathing.

"Do you want to try?"

"Sure."

"Perfect. Come sit next to me." Devika patted the couch.

"How should I sit? Because I don't think my legs work like yours."

"Just sit comfortably. Sit up straight and relax your arms."

"Okay."

"Good. Now we're going to breathe. Just follow me."

Brad followed Devika's instructions as she guided him through the meditation.

After she brought him out of it, she asked, "How do you feel?"

"Incredible, actually. I feel relaxed. My old pastor had no idea what he was talking about."

Devika frowned. "Yeah, what a surprise," she muttered.

"Thank you for teaching me. I found it enjoyable."

"Well, I'm glad you liked it. One nice thing about meditation is how you can do it anywhere, at any time. I can text you some resources if you want."

"I'd appreciate anything you send me. Thank you."

"You're welcome." Devika nodded toward the pile of Ikea packaging refuse. "We should probably bag up any styrofoam before we leave."

"Good call."

They quickly tidied up the place before leaving. Brad escorted Devika to his pickup truck, which she eyed disapprovingly.

"Do you get miles per gallon, or gallons per mile in this thing?"

"In my defense, I'm from Eastern Oregon. Every boy is issued one of these with his driver's license. It's the law." Brad smiled to show he was joking.

Devika smirked and responded wryly, "A penis pump would be cheaper."

"*Ouch.* That hurts."

Her smirk widened into a grin. "So I hear."

"What? Hey, I've never used one of those."

"A pickup truck or penis pump?" Devika was flat-out laughing now.

Brad recognized his defeat and changed tactics. "Would it help to mention that I take public transportation to work?"

"Actually, yes. On the plus side, if I ever need help setting up an Indian wedding, I know the guy to call."

"Why, is there a lot of stuff involved?"

Devika nodded ruefully. "You have no idea. I'm guessing you've never been to an Indian wedding?"

"I can't say I have."

"Seen one in a movie?"

"Nope."

"Well, I've been to a bunch, including my own. It's a marathon. A very beautiful and grueling marathon."

"Is there food?"

"Pfft. What do you think? Mountains of it."

"Cool. I'll be your plus-one for the next one, so long as there's a buffet."

Devika gave him a strange look, then chuckled. "I'll think about it." She looked at the truck. "Do you have a ladder, or should I get my climbing gear?"

"Sorry. I can give—"

"I'm teasing. Just unlock it. I can get in myself. I'm glad I'm in yoga pants and not a skirt, or else your neighbors would get the full monty."

There's a naughty image. I'm not sure how to follow that up, so I'll just unlock the door.

Brad bought more than he planned for at the pet store—Devika seemed to pop a new cat toy into the cart every time he turned his head. At the checkout line, he shook his head ruefully, saying, "I'm never going shopping with you again. You're worse than Sophia."

Devika pouted at him.

"Sophia has a better pout, too."

Devika sniffed, crossed her arms, and looked away.

He chortled. "In my defense, it's very difficult to out pout an eight-year-old."

Brad could feel the excitement building as he drove up to the shelter. The same volunteer as yesterday was there. "Welcome back. Do you want to interact with Cricket again?"

"Yes, please."

Brad and Devika sat on a bench in the tiny room. While they waited, Devika asked, "Are you sure about getting a cat on Christmas Eve? Aren't you going to be away for Christmas?"

"I'm here for Christmas. Alone. I don't want to see my parents because—that's a long story. Sophia is in Portland spending Christmas with Megan and Tasha." The pathetic recitation of his loneliness left Brad feeling dejected.

Before either of them could say more, the volunteer reappeared with Cricket in her arms. She set the cat down on the ground. Cricket looked around alertly before hopping onto the bench between Brad and Devika. She headbutted Brad, and he started petting her. His mood improved the moment his hand touched her soft fur.

My life might be a steaming pile of shit right now, but this little girl makes everything seem better. If Cricket can be abandoned and still survive and find a new life with me, then I can deal with the consequences of my own actions and find my own new way.

They could hear her purrs as both humans petted and scratched her.

"Look, Brad. She's smiling."

He peered at her little face. "She is." His fingers brushed against Devika's as they continued pampering Cricket. "And I am, too."

Brad started the adoption process shortly thereafter. Once he signed the documents and paid the fees, the volunteer handed over Cricket with warm thanks. His poor little girl cried nervously inside the carrier, so he spoke words of reassurance as he carried her out. Brad felt a tiny pang of loss when he handed Cricket to Devika once she was settled in the truck. As he pulled himself into the driver's seat, he saw her hunched over the carrier, cooing softly. He smiled as he drove in silence, listening to Devika's gentle murmurs. She grudgingly handed Cricket down so he could carry her into her new home. He set the carrier down and watched Cricket slowly emerge, her tail twitching rapidly.

"I'm gonna go. See you soon, Brad."

"Thanks for coming with me today on this wild journey. And thank you for being so kind with Cricket. I'm sure she appreciated hearing you talk to her. Today was a great day."

"It was, and you're welcome."

"Are you sure you don't want to stay for a bit?"

"No, I need to go."

Devika shut the door. Brad walked to the couch and sat down. Cricket joined him and snuggled in tight. He cast a wistful glance at the door before running his fingers across his new companion's warm and soft fur. The vibrations from her purrs flowed into his body and burrowed into his soul, filling him with warm, syrupy joy.

Chapter 10
Kashmir
Led Zeppelin

Devika could feel tears welling in her eyes. Brad's little cat was adorable.

The way Brad looked at Cricket. He's totally in love with her. I'm happy for him. I just wish seeing a grown man snuggling a cat didn't make me feel sorry for myself. Manny is right—I need to open myself up to love. I wish I knew how. Did I ever know how to be open?

At least I'm having a good day, even if I'm crying in the rain. Yoga was good, shopping was fun, and helping Brad adopt a cat was awesome. I wonder if I can cat-sit for him? Those good feelings should outweigh the loneliness, right?

What if I asked Brad out? He's single. We keep having these not-a-dates. Pros and cons. Pro—we get along. Con—he just got divorced, and I don't want to be the rebound chick. Pro—we share an interest in yoga. Con—he started off by being an arrogant alpha male moron. Pro—he gets along with Manny and Nelson. Con—he's clearly working through some religious baggage. Which means maybe he isn't as cool with Manny and Nelson as he seems. Pro—he's kinda hot. Con—he can't cook, and I suspect Megan had to do a lot around the house. Speaking of Megan, why did they get divorced? I keep assuming it's because she's a lesbian and is sleeping with her best friend, but what is the actual reason? Why is he in Seattle? Brad says it's for a job, but I can't believe he couldn't get a job in Portland where he would be close to Sophia.

Cons win. Also, I need to find out more. Brad has too many mysteries.

At home, Devika started cooking. Tomorrow was a big day, and good Indian food took time to prepare. She started yesterday and foolishly cost herself hours today. There was plenty of time, though—provided she was efficient.

Mummy would be appalled that I'm not listening to traditional Indian music while I prepare the food, but it doesn't call to me. If Mummy wanted a good Indian girl, then she should have sent me to live with my aunties in Mumbai. Instead, she raised me in America, so now I cook while listening to Green Day and Led Zeppelin. And unlike a good Indian girl, I divorced my gay, upper-caste husband, disgracing our family. They might have forgiven me if I'd at least managed to get a few kids out of it.

Devika took a break to meditate, letting go of her negative feelings. Re-centered, she resumed cooking. Devika never measured, guided by experience, instinct, and passion. She celebrated the culinary legacy of her ancestors to the rhythm of rock and roll.

Christmas morning dawned chilly and damp, as was typical for Seattle. The day meant nothing to her, but every year, Nelson threw an all-day party for anyone who wanted to come, anyone who was alone. Ever since Manny and Nelson started dating, this was Devika's favorite event of the year. The timing this year was perfect because she had Saturday and Sunday to cook. She stuffed her car full of food and drove to Nelson's penthouse condo. He groggily admitted her before summoning Manny to help her unload. With Nelson's kitchen commandeered, Devika got to work heating things up and cooking any dishes which needed to be made the same day.

She hummed to herself as she cooked, dancing around Manny and Nelson as they fixed coffee and breakfast for themselves. As the two men prepared for their day, they drifted in and out of the kitchen, admiring the looks and smells of Devika's efforts. She knew there would be pizza and burgers available—this was America, after all—but today's guests would also be able to taste the best of India.

As the first guests were arriving, Nelson interrupted her flow. "What's Brad doing today?"

Chapter 11

Missing You

John Waite

Brad tried not to think about what day it was. Cricket was living up to her name, chirping hungrily as he staggered into the kitchen. He took half a can of food out of the fridge and mixed it with some dry food in her bowl. He didn't mix it well, because Cricket was standing on the counter with her head pressed firmly inside her bowl as he tried to work. Brad gave up on mixing and refilled her water bowl. He went about taking care of the rest of Cricket's needs before finding something to eat for himself.

After an uninspiring breakfast of toast, Brad took a shower and sat down on the couch to read. Cricket walked up to him and headbutted him. Brad petted her, but she remained frustratingly insistent on something he wasn't providing.

"Are you trying to get under the blanket?"

Cricket chirped.

Brad lifted the blanket covering his legs, and Cricket crawled underneath. She made her way on top of his legs and curled up. She was soft, fuzzy, and very warm. Her chirp shifted to a purr, and finally, a tiny little snore. Brad smiled and picked up his book.

His legs were starting to cramp when his phone notified him of an incoming FaceTime. He opened the app to see his smiling daughter.

"Hi, Daddy! Merry Christmas!" Sophia waved at him. Brad waved back.

"Merry Christmas to you, pumpkin. Has Santa been good to you?"

"I'm old enough to know there's no such thing as Santa!"

"There's not? If there's no Santa, then how did my present get to you?"

"The mail, duh!"

Brad chuckled at the sharp wit of his daughter.

"All right. You got me."

"Thank you for my present!" Brad had gotten her a gift card from Five Stride Skate Shop for her roller derby gear. "Mommy and Mama Tasha are taking me next week!"

"That's wonderful, Sophia." Brad paused. "Sophia, I want you to meet someone." He held the camera back and lifted the blanket to reveal Cricket curled into a little ball on his legs.

"Daddy! You got a cat!"

Brad could hear Megan in the background say, "What did you say? Brad has a cat?" Suddenly Megan and Tasha appeared behind Sophia.

"Everyone, meet Cricket."

There was a chorus of cooing from the other side of the call.

"I brought her home yesterday from the shelter. She's super sweet."

Sophia asked, "Why is her name Cricket?"

"She was abandoned by her previous family and survived by eating crickets. A real estate agent brought her to the shelter, and they named her Cricket."

Megan interjected, "That's a weird name, given she used to eat crickets."

"True. But I like it anyway," Brad replied.

"How's your Christmas?" Megan asked.

Brad paused. "Sophia, can I talk to your mom?"

"Yes, Daddy!"

"It was good seeing you, pumpkin. Merry Christmas. I love you."

"I love you, too! Merry Christmas, Daddy!"

Brad choked up a bit as Tasha led Sophia away. Once she was out of earshot, he answered Megan's question. "My Christmas sucks." Brad lowered his voice. "I realize it's my fault for being an asshole. Or as Tasha so eloquently put it, a homewrecking skank."

"I'm sorry, Brad. Maybe after the wounds have healed we can do something together some Christmas."

"I'd like to, even though I don't deserve it. How is your Christmas?"

Megan smiled fondly. "Quiet, cozy, and sweet. We had hot chocolate and opened presents. It's strange, though. Sophia misses you."

"I miss her a lot. Honestly, I miss all of the family stuff I took for granted. I'm grateful for Cricket. She's helping me get through."

"You haven't heard from your girlfriend?"

Brad chuckled ruefully. "We're not dating. We went shopping for cat stuff, and she helped me bring Cricket home yesterday, but, no, I haven't heard from her today."

Megan looked skeptical. "She went shopping and cat adopting with you, but you're not dating?"

"We're not dating. I swear. Devika and I are yoga buddies."

"Uh-huh. Yoga buddies." Megan paused. "Just curious—I've never heard the name Devika before."

"She was born in the U.S., but her parents immigrated from India."

"Uh-huh." She looked skeptical.

"Thursday, after class, she introduced me to Indian food."

"Uh-huh."

"It was amazing."

"Uh-huh."

"Megan, you're weirding me out."

"I'm just processing, Brad. Let me get this straight. Your Indian-American yoga buddy has gone out with you for Indian food.

Which, I might remind you, you refused to eat when I tried to make it. You've been to multiple classes with her. She also went shopping with you and helped you adopt a cat. *But,* you aren't dating?"

"When you say it all together, it sounds weird, but we aren't dating."

"Do you not find her attractive or something?"

"Uh. It feels strange talking with you about this."

Megan grunted. "*No shit, Brad.* I can't believe we're having this conversation, but somehow, here we are. You didn't answer the question."

"Devika is very attractive. She's smart, and wickedly funny. But we're just yoga buddies."

"*Right.*"

"Hey, I'm getting a call."

"Devika?" Her eyebrow went up.

He looked at Megan, chagrined. "Yeah."

"Merry Christmas, Brad. Say hi to your not-a-girlfriend for me." Megan stuck her tongue out and ended the connection.

Brad fumbled with his phone and answered before the call went to voicemail.

"Hi, yoga buddy," Devika greeted him with a bubbly voice.

"Hi." Brad paused, feeling self-conscious after his discussion with Megan. "Yoga buddy."

"I'm calling because Nelson does this thing every Christmas where he invites people who don't have any family nearby or who don't celebrate Christmas to come to his place for a casual get-to-gether. Do you want to come over?"

"Sure, so long as I can get home to feed Cricket."

"It's casual. Come and go as you please."

"Great. When does it start?"

"It just did. I'll text you Nelson's address."

"Thanks, see you soon."

"Bye now."

Brad looked at the cat ball in his lap. "Okay, Cricket. I need to get up and change into real clothes."

Cricket chirped in protest but quickly settled into the nook of the couch to sleep.

Chapter 12

Miss Mystery

Black & Blue

Devika put down her phone to half-heartedly glare at Nelson. "Happy now?"

"You can't be upset with me. The entire point of this party is to give lonely people a place to gather and have fun."

She sighed. "I'm not upset with you. Did Manny put you up to this?"

Nelson looked confused. "No. Why?"

"We agreed he would stop trying to set me up with men if I opened myself up to love. Whatever that means."

Eyebrows raised, Nelson leaned forward over the kitchen counter. "Does this mean you have feelings about Brad?"

"No! We're just friends. We see each other at yoga. That's it."

I sound defensive. It's true, though. I already went through the pros and cons about this.

"All right. You're just friends. Did he say when he's coming?"

"Soon?"

Nelson looked at the food displayed in front of him. "You've outdone yourself again. This looks and smells incredible."

"Thank you."

"Why don't I start moving the hot items to the buffet warmers while you get changed?"

"I can help."

"You've done more than enough, Devika. I'll get Manny to help. Shoo. Get changed." He gently harried her out of the kitchen.

Devika walked into Nelson and Manny's bedroom, retrieving her bag, which Manny had placed on the bed during the unloading process. She took it into their bathroom and started changing.

By the time she emerged, the party was going. There was a cluster of people around the football game on Nelson's gigantic television, while another small group huddled out on the balcony. On a good day, the view from the balcony was spectacular. Late December weather in the Pacific Northwest rarely qualified as good, and the balcony had no protection from the wind and rain. Devika could see the thicker puffs of smoke contrasting with the thin clouds of breath.

I'm so glad I've never smoked or vaped. Those poor bastards must be freezing. Let me see how the food is going. Surveying what was left, she estimated what more was needed. *I'll prepare more* samosas *and* naan.

Manny and Nelson intercepted her on her way to the kitchen. Her ex-husband whistled appreciatively. "Seriously, Devika? You didn't look this good at the gala. I'm jealous."

"Jealous? Jealous of what?"

He pursed his lips and gave her a hurt look before answering. "Jealous of whom. I'm wondering who might be the beneficiary of your efforts."

"Stop. I put a lot less effort into this than I did for the gala."

"And yet you look more beautiful. What do you think, Nelson?"

"I saw the photos from the gala, and Manny's right. You look even more gorgeous today."

Devika sniffed. "I have no idea what you're talking about. This isn't even a new *sari*."

Nelson looked unconvinced. "You look good enough to make me consider being straight."

Manny slapped his arm.

"Not that I would, of course." He leaned over to kiss Manny with tender appreciation. "I'm already taken."

They are cute together. Hopefully, Manny likes his New Year's surprise.

Devika harrumphed at them. "Out of my way. I need to refill the *naan* and *samosas*."

Manny frowned. "Fine, but don't spend all day in the kitchen. Enjoy yourself."

"I will. Now shoo." Devika waved her hands emphatically at the men until they moved.

She refilled the *samosas* and *naan*, and she was working through a back-up batch of *naan* when she sensed she wasn't alone. She looked over her shoulder to see Brad leaning against the wall.

He does look good, even in just jeans, t-shirt, and a flannel shirt. Is he checking out my ass?

"What? You're just standing there like a creeper and not saying hi?"

"Sorry, I didn't want to interrupt your flow. Hi, by the way."

"Hi, yourself. Stop staring at me and be useful."

"I wasn't staring."

The guilty blush on your face says otherwise.

"Here, take this." Devika handed Brad a bowl and pastry brush. "Use the brush to spread garlic butter on these *naan*." She pointed to a plate of cooked *naan*.

He chuckled. "Thank you for giving me a task within my skill set. Your dress is beautiful."

"It's not a dress. It's a *sari*."

"Oh, I—"

"You'll be sorry you don't know what a *sari* is." She didn't bother to hide the mirth in her tone.

Brad chuckled at her pun. "Yes, I'm already sorry."

"A dress is clothing with a seam. A *sari* is a single piece of cloth wrapped around me."

"Wait, you're wearing a wrap?"

"Yep. No zipper or seams."

I can see him trying to figure out how this works, especially the bare midriff.

"What about the top?"

"The top is called a choli. It keeps me from flashing my boobs at everyone."

"Uh."

I probably shouldn't have said boobs. I might have broken his brain.

"Brad, the garlic butter..."

"Right. Sorry. I got distracted."

She couldn't contain a slight snicker. "I can't imagine why."

He graciously ignored her dig. "Thank you for telling me about *saris*."

"Oh, Brad," Devika sighed. "We barely scratched the surface. *Saris* have been an integral part of India's culture for thousands of years. When I got married, I wore a red *sari*, because red is a traditional marriage color. If I'm in mourning, I would wear a white *sari*."

"*Saris* sound complicated."

"They are and they aren't. The colors and how a *sari* is worn vary across India. We have more cultures and subcultures than we do languages."

Manny was apparently eavesdropping, because he added, "I have to be honest, Devika looks more beautiful today than she did in her red wedding *sari*."

Devika sighed. "How's the food situation, Manny?"

"We're low on rice."

"I figured. I'll have another batch ready in about five minutes."

"You're amazing." He inclined his head toward their guest. "Brad, how are you?"

"I'm good. How 'bout you?"

"Wonderful. I love this party. I hear you have a new cat."

"I do. I guess Devika told you."

"She did." Manny paused for a beat before changing the subject. "Did you have a chance to talk to your daughter today?"

Damn. I should have asked Brad that question.

"I did! Best part of my day. We did one of those video chats, and I showed her Cricket."

"Was she excited?"

"Very. She was adorable. Then my ex and her girlfriend had to see Cricket as well."

Devika interjected, "How was seeing your ex?"

"It was awkward, but getting better. Megan says hi, by the way."

Her heart suddenly beat a bit faster. "To me?"

"Yeah."

She felt her eyes narrow. "What exactly did you tell *your ex-wife* about me?"

He looks like he realized he might have stepped in it. Manny's face appears as if he's about ready to explode with curiosity.

Brad took an uncomfortable breath. "I told her we are friends and yoga buddies."

"I see," she said flatly.

Devika could see the panic on Brad's features. He sounded desperate when he asked, "Um, so you two never had kids?"

Manny laughed heartily. Devika was too shocked to say anything, so Manny answered first. "Devika really wanted kids, but let's just say that most of our sex wasn't where kids go."

I'm going to murder him. Slowly and painfully.

Brad stood there, clearly trying to process what he'd heard.

"Manmeet? Can I speak with you *right now*? Excuse us, Brad."

Devika grabbed Manny and hauled him into the bedroom. "What the *fuck* were you thinking, telling Brad anything about our sex lives?"

"I thought it would be funny," Manny said sheepishly. "I'm sorry."

"You're damn right you're sorry. Go find Nelson or something, because I can't be around you right now."

"I'm really sorry, Devika."

She sighed. "I know you didn't mean any harm. I'm just pissed right now and need some space."

"All right."

Devika stalked back to the kitchen and pulled the last *naan* off the frying pan before it got too crispy. She noted Brad quietly buttering the *naan*, giving her space.

"I'm sorry about Manny. Sometimes he doesn't think."

"I understand. I'm no stranger to not thinking and then screwing up royally because of it."

They kept busy in awkward silence. Devika sighed deeply. "You really want to ask me what he meant, don't you."

She could see the tension melt out of Brad's body. "Yes. I'm sorry, but now I'm curious."

Devika looked around to make sure no one could hear them. "Fine. I can't believe I'm about to tell you this." She looked Brad straight in the eye. "If you tell anyone what I'm about to divulge, I swear to you no one will *ever* find your body."

"I promise I won't tell anyone."

"We didn't have sex after our wedding night. We fought about it a lot. About a year into our marriage, Manny admitted he was gay. So, I spent the next year trying to cure him." She added air quotes around "cure." Devika felt blood rushing to her cheeks.

"Cure him how?"

"Lots of sex."

"But you said—"

"Yeah. I thought I could entice him to have sex with me as a woman if I did things with him like a man."

"You mean—"

"Yeah."

"Wow. I see why you were so pissed off with him for saying what he did. So, what happened? Because obviously you didn't make him straight."

"No. After about a year, I realized it wasn't working. Eventually, I just accepted he was gay, and we weren't having kids."

Bless his heart. He looks concerned.

"Are you okay with not having children? Do you want them?"

"Honestly, I don't know anymore. I really wanted kids because I wanted to be the good Indian daughter married to an upper caste man. Now, I don't give a shit about being the dutiful girl. I'm not sure where that leaves me. Maybe I would want kids with the right guy. I know I don't want to be a single mother."

"Makes sense. Single parenting is terrifying. I'm so grateful Megan has Tasha."

He looks so sad.

"Do you need a hug?"

Devika could see the unspoken relief on his face. "Please."

She brought Brad into an embrace. He was so tense. After a few seconds, he rested his head on her shoulder. Devika could feel the tension slowly draining from his body as their embrace extended. She felt some of her own tension evaporating into the ether. It had been so long since she'd held someone and been held in turn. The simple human contact felt good.

What do I feel down there? Is he...?

Brad suddenly pulled back, his cheeks blushing. "Um, thanks, Devika. I really needed a hug." The pitch of his voice crept upward as he stuttered, "Isn't the rice about done? Let me get this *naan* out there. Bye!" And he scuttled off with the *naan*, leaving Devika alone in the kitchen.

Yep, I felt his dick. It's been a long time since I've had one of those. I'm good with the hug, though.

She took the rice out to the buffet table and grabbed a mojito from the pitcher on the bar. Sipping her drink, she went and stood with Nelson near the football game. They clinked glasses and stood in companionable silence as they watched the game.

Chapter 13

Gonna Make You Sweat (Everybody Dance Now)

C+C Music Factory

Brad hung out until late afternoon, doing his best to avoid Devika. He did eat her food, which shifted throughout the day. There was always rice, *naan*, and *samosas*, and she made a number of meat and vegetarian dishes which rotated through the buffet table as the day wore on. Her food was so good that he skipped the burgers and pizza. The kitchen became a hotspot, with a gaggle of partygoers in there constantly. Brad mostly hung out at the board game table or the football game.

I can't believe I was getting hard during our hug. It was so inappropriate. She was being kind, and it felt so good to touch another person. Then He had to get involved. I just want to tell her it was involuntary. What if she didn't notice, and I say something? Would it be better or worse if she didn't notice? I honestly don't know which I prefer. Either way, I'm just not going to mention anything.

He took a break during halftime to load up a plate of Devika's cooking before returning to the game. The teams were preparing for the second-half kickoff when a beer bottle obscured his vision. Glancing up, he saw Nelson smiling at him. Brad took the proffered bottle.

"Thanks, Nelson."

"You're quite welcome." He nodded at Brad's plate. "Not a fan of pizza?"

"Dude, I love pizza, but I can have pizza anytime. This—" He waved his fork at his overloaded plate. "Holy shit, this is amazing. I can happily skip pizza for home-cooked Indian food any time."

Nelson chuckled. "When Manny and I first started dating, I felt somewhat threatened by his close relationship with his soon-to-be ex-wife. Then, Devika invited me over for dinner one night, and I realized three things. First, she's a great person. Second, she's an excellent cook. And third, I was going to need to start exercising to burn off the calories."

Brad threw his head back and laughed. "Right on all three counts. I'm going to have to go hiking or jogging or something after today."

Before he left, Brad made sure to say goodbye to Devika, Manny, and Nelson. Once home, he went on a walk around the neighborhood before he fed Cricket, who acted like she had never eaten before. After her dinner, they played with her string toys, and she leapt around, chasing them. Her antics kept him wildly amused. He especially enjoyed watching her do an excited little butt wiggle right before she pounced. When Cricket finally tired, Brad opened up a meditation video and started meditating. Cricket crawled into his lap while he found his center.

Over the next two days, Brad didn't see Devika at yoga. Their schedules didn't mesh on Tuesday, and she had the intermediate class on Wednesday. Thursday, he wouldn't see her either, because he was going to the Kraken game with Nelson.

Brad brought his Kraken jersey to work, changing right before he left. He took transit down to the arena, texting Nelson with updates. The two met at a sports bar under the long shadow of the Space Needle. Brad shook hands with the taller man when they met, then headed inside. The place was packed, but Brad managed to snag two seats at the bar.

"All right. Can you explain hockey to me?" Nelson asked.

"Honestly, probably not. I can cover the basics, but there's a lot you will just have to see. Feel free to ask questions, though."

"My first question then is about this." Nelson gestured at the crowded sports bar, which was quickly getting overcrowded.

Brad grinned. "A sports bar is often part of the experience. Let's order real fast and then we can talk."

The two quickly perused the menus. Brad considered the burger, but went with a chicken sandwich instead. Nelson ordered the same thing. They each ordered a pint as well.

"Nelson, you have to understand how food and sports are inextricably linked in American culture. Whether it's sports bars or tailgating before a game, this is who we are."

"So, greasy food is part of sports." He continued with a chuckle, "That seems counterintuitive. Also, what is tailgating?"

"Well, *fried* food is part of the sports experience. Athletes probably shouldn't eat like this. Tailgating is a phenomenon where people bring trucks or campers and set up grills and stuff. It becomes a social thing. Sports bars are like tailgating, with less chance of rain. We eat, drink, and talk about the upcoming game. We talk about our team and the opponents."

"What do you talk about?"

"That's a complex question. There are different types of sports fans. Okay, see the angry-looking guy over there?" Brad indicated a loud young man shouting at the others at his table.

"I see him."

"He's the eternal optimist. He always thinks his team is going to win. If they lose, then they will win the next game. Or the next season."

"Why is he shouting?"

"See the other guy at the table? The red-faced one?"

"Right."

"He's the doomsayer. He loves the team with all of his heart, but he thinks management sucks, or the coaches. Maybe he thinks the players don't do the right things. The doomsayer is sure the team is going to lose."

Nelson looked puzzled. "But he still comes?"

"Oh, yeah. Life is great for a doomsayer. If your team wins, then that's great. If your team loses, then you still have a positive feeling because your prediction was correct."

"So strange, but it makes sense. I encountered much of the same among cricket fans in Kenya."

"See, we're all the same," Brad exclaimed.

Well, there's some personal growth. I'm hanging out in a sports bar with a gay Black man. Two things I wouldn't have done a couple of months ago. Nelson's a good dude, and this is fun. Finding our commonality is what's important.

"What kind of fan are you, Brad?"

"I like to think of myself as a hopeful realist. The Kraken are doing okay this season. We're sitting in the middle of the standings right now. I'm pretty sure we aren't winning the Stanley Cup this year, but I'm hopeful for the future. Things will get interesting soon, though."

"Why?"

"We're just a couple months away from the trade deadline, and I don't know which way we'll go. Are we going to try to get some veterans and make a run for the playoffs, or will we trade off some of our established talent, hopefully picking up younger players who might pay off later?"

Nelson considered this. "That is a dilemma. Do you have a preference?"

Brad shook his head. "Dude, that's always a hard question. My heart wants them to make a run for the playoffs. Roll the dice and hope for the best. My head wants them to gear up for another year.

My heart hates that, because trading for the future usually means parting with players I like."

Nelson clapped him on the back, laughing. "I understand completely, my friend."

The two chatted as they ate their chicken sandwiches. Nelson paid for their meal since Brad got the tickets. Once inside the arena, they settled in about ten rows off the ice.

"These look like good seats," Nelson observed.

"I got lucky. I wanted your first hockey experience to be down here in the lower bowl. The tickets are pricey, but it's worth it. The game is *much* faster the closer you are to the ice."

"Thank you. I look forward to this."

"You're welcome. We're also in the corner behind the visitor's net, so we'll see the Kraken shooting twice on this end. They'll defend this net in the second period."

"Wonderful." Nelson looked over at Brad. "Would you be willing to do me a favor?"

"Uh, sure. What is it?"

"My firm throws a New Year's Eve party every year. We celebrate the firm's successes and the people who made it possible. It's a big event for us." Nelson paused. "I plan to propose to Manny at the stroke of midnight."

"Oh, wow. Does he know?"

"Not unless Devika told him."

"She's in on the plan, then?"

"Yes. Unfortunately, Manny decided to pick her up on the way. I need another co-conspirator to get Devika's camera and some other items in place. Would you be willing to assist me?"

Now I'm about to help two gay men get married. There's a good chance my old pastor would have me stoned to death in the church parking lot. Tasha was right. I really did need to find a better flavor of Christianity.

"Of course, Nelson. Just tell me what you need from me."

Nelson flashed him a huge smile. "Thank you so much."

They enjoyed the game, an experience made better because the Kraken won. Brad wasn't sure if Nelson fully understood the game, but he seemed to have fun.

Cricket greeted him excitedly when he got home. Brad was happy to see her, too. He apologized to the cat for her late dinner, but she seemed to forgive him, tucking herself under the covers and behind his knees when he clambered into bed.

Chapter 14

Would I Lie To You?

Eurythmics

Devika didn't see Brad again until Sunday morning, New Year's Eve. In the brief minutes between the beginner and intermediate classes, she handed off her camera and a small jewelry box to Brad.

"It's great seeing you again," she said. "I'm sorry it's been so busy since the party."

"No worries. I've been slammed at work because everyone's out. I've been meaning to tell you how much I loved your cooking."

She laughed. "I heard. Nelson told me you skipped pizza."

"I did, and it was worth it."

"Thank you. I appreciate the compliment. Anyway, my class is about to start. Take good care of the box and my camera." She flashed him a stern look. "If anything happens to either, there will be no place on Earth you can hide."

He chuckled. "I will guard them with my life. I'll assign my fiercest guard cat to the task."

She rolled her eyes. "See you tonight, and say hi to Cricket for me."

"Will do."

She would have liked to chat longer, but the timing was poor. As she waved goodbye to Brad, she reviewed tonight's scheme in her head. Devika wanted Manny's night to be perfect. She had a mani-pedi scheduled at noon—likely the last relaxation she would get until after midnight.

Damn Manny for being so nice. I'll make this work. Brad better do his part. Maybe we can talk discreetly about his not-so-little pants incident at the party and why he avoided me afterward.

Devika was meditating when Manny texted to inform her that they were almost at her apartment. She slipped on her strappy-heeled sandals and went to meet Manny.

"Damn, Devika. Is Nelson setting you up with someone at the party?"

"No. Can't a girl just look nice?"

"Sure, but you don't look nice. You are multiple steps *beyond* nice."

"Thanks, I think. Happy New Year's, Nelson."

Nelson glanced back from the driver's seat and replied, "Happy New Year. You do look smashing tonight."

I can't believe I put in this much effort to look good for my ex-husband's engagement.

"Thank you both. You can stop with the compliments. Also, you both look nice."

They smiled at her from the front seat. Nelson drove them to his firm's building, parking in his private spot. They rode the elevator to the top floor, exiting into the firm's conference and executive level. The decorations were spot on, and there was already a line at the bar.

Nelson boomed, "There's my last guest."

Devika saw Brad turn to greet them, drink in hand.

Oh, damn. He cleans up really nice, and I do love a man in a tux. Just a hint of five o'clock shadow. Mmm. Did he get a haircut? Why is he staring? Oh. Me. He's staring at me.

Devika smiled ferally adding a subtle sway to her hips as she glided forward. "Hello, Mr. Kowalski. It's lovely to see you tonight." She held out her hand to shake his, but was surprised when he lifted it to his lips for a soft kiss.

"Good evening, Ms. Kumar. You look enchanting tonight."

Oh my god, he's practically purring. And I better look fantastic in this sari. *It cost a small fortune.*

"Why, thank you. That tux looks good on you."

"Royal blue and gold are perfect on you. Are those real gemstones?"

"Shh, a girl doesn't tell all her secrets."

"I'll have to see what I can do to get you to open up."

"And just how do you plan on...opening me up?" Devika asked coquettishly.

"I'm thinking I might drop to my knees and beg."

There's his deep rumbly purr again. Oh, shit. I think I just got wet.

Devika sniffed airily. "Begging might work, but first, I would like a drink."

"I have a mojito for you." Brad handed her a glass from the high boy behind him.

"How did you—"

"It was your drink of choice at Christmas."

He noticed and remembered.

"Strange, Manny. He didn't get drinks for us."

"I just noticed that, Nelson. I suppose we simply aren't important enough."

"Well, I suppose we must wait in line, by ourselves."

"I'm not sure. Do you think it's safe to leave my gorgeous ex-wife unattended?"

For a minute, I forgot Manny and Nelson were even here. Get a grip on yourself and stop flirting.

"Never fear, gentlemen. I promise to safeguard her honor in your absence."

Devika sniffed at the men's antics. "I can bloody well safeguard my own honor." She stalked off toward the windows, ostensibly to look at the Seattle skyline. In the glass, she could see Brad slowly following her. She smiled inwardly, noting how he was staring at her reflection, not her ass.

I wouldn't blame him if he did.

"I'm sorry if—"

"Shh. You three boys aren't the only ones who can dish bullshit." She grinned at his reflection. "Please tell me you own your own tux."

Brad shifted awkwardly from one foot to the other before responding, "I got married in this tux ten and a half years ago. Haven't worn it since."

"It still fits nicely. Wearing your wedding tuxedo is an interesting choice."

"Nelson is proposing tonight, so I wanted to look the part."

"As did I."

"You fucking nailed it. Sorry about the language."

"My delicate ears can take it." Devika smirked at his reflection. She could see his fingers twitching. "You can touch it if you want."

Brad's reflected hands moved slowly toward her. She watched his mouth open in a silent 'O' as he gently rubbed the fabric. "Is this—"

"Silk."

"Holy shit. How much did this cost?"

Half my savings, but damn is it worth it. Every time I move, it's like wearing an orgasm.

"Remember what I told you about girls and their secrets." Her tone was scolding, but there was no force behind it. "Speaking of secrets, why are you really here, Brad?"

He looked confused. "Nelson invited me. You know, for the thing later tonight."

"No, why are you in Seattle? The honest reason." Devika watched his face crumble in the reflection.

"*Fuck*. Can we go over there?" Brad nodded toward an empty space. They walked over to a high boy and settled in. "Fuck. I could use another drink or five for this."

"I'm sorry I asked. You can tell me to fuck off, and it's none of my business."

Brad puffed his cheeks out and blew out a breath through pursed lips. "No, it's okay. If we're going to be friends, then you need to know. Then you can decide if you still want to be my friend afterward."

What the fuck?

He sighed, and started. "Megan left me when she caught me screwing another woman in our bed. She took Sophia and fled to Portland. Tasha gave them a place to stay. As they reconnected, they discovered they loved each other."

"You cheated on Megan."

"I did." Brad's eyes were focused on the table between them, unable to look her in the eyes. "Again."

"Again?" Devika could hear the brittleness in her voice.

"The first time was nine years ago."

Devika did the math in her head. "While Megan was pregnant?"

"Yeah. In case you ever wondered how much of an asshole I am."

I have no idea what to say.

"I fucked up my entire life. That's why I'm in Seattle. I needed space. Space to get away from my father, who I've realized is a monster. Space away from Megan and Sophia, because they need to find happiness. Finally, I needed space to find out if I can stop being an asshole."

Brad looked up, finally. Devika saw the pain and guilt etched in his eyes. She could see him withdrawing, shutting down. To her own surprise, she reached out and touched his hand. Startled, he looked at her.

"Anything else?"

"Fuck it. I was a shitty father and husband. I spent too much time at work. I wasn't there for Megan and Sophia. I was distant and unattached. Again, I'm an asshole."

Devika breathed in. "Brad, let's do our breathing exercises, okay. Just follow me."

She led them in breathing exercises for a couple of minutes as she gathered her thoughts and feelings.

"Thank you for being honest. I can't imagine how much speaking your truth sucked."

He nodded ruefully.

"There's a lot to unpack. I need time to process this. How do you feel?"

"Awful. Like I ruined everything all over again." He drew in a deep breath. "Also, better. Like I don't have any secrets anymore. I hated hiding who I am from you."

They stood there in silence, sipping at their drinks and stealing glances at the skyline beyond the windows.

Devika broke the silence. "I don't think you were hiding who you are. You might have been hiding who you were, but not who you are."

"I don't get it."

"Let's be honest. Going to your first yoga class like you did was a dick move, and you've definitely had your bad moments, *but* you've also had some good moments, too. You're a work in progress, Brad. We all are."

"I'm really trying to be a better person. Like I told you before, I promised Megan I would be a father Sophia could be proud of. I'm done with being a homewrecking skank."

Devika snorted before she could stop herself. "What?"

"Tasha called me that. It's true, but I vowed not to let it be anymore."

"I need to meet this Tasha person."

"Please no. I might not survive."

"Can I ask you something, Brad?"

"Sure, why not." He sounded defeated.

"Have you been with anyone since Megan caught you?"

"No. No one, I swear."

"You're not on some hook-up app now, looking for randoms to bang?"

"I promised Tasha the next person I slept with would be someone I would be proud to have her meet Sophia."

"You promised *Tasha* that?"

"It's a long story, but yeah. I made the promise, and I'm sticking with it."

"Can I tell you something? Something about me?"

"Sure."

I can't believe I'm doing this. He's been honest with me, so I might as well be honest with him in turn.

"After Manny found Nelson, and I decided to divorce him, I went through a slut phase. I hadn't had sex with anything not silicone in years, my parents fucking hated me, I was getting divorced, and my life felt like a total fucking failure. I was angry, depressed, and in a bad place. So, I filled the emptiness and negativity in my life with a lot of sex. Some of it was good, most of it was bad."

"Oh. Wow."

"There's something else. I'm allergic to the pill. Well, not allergic, but we don't get along. So, for about six months, I made some really bad decisions. I mean, *really bad* decisions. Not even Manny and Nelson know about this part of my life. Honestly, it's a goddamn miracle I'm not a single mother. So yeah, I understand making poor choices."

"We both gave each other a lot to unpack tonight, didn't we?"

"You're putting it mildly. Brad, I respect your intention and efforts to be better. I've been there."

"Can I ask you something?"

"Might as well, since we're in a sharing mood."

"You said you slept around for six months. What about after those six months?"

"Once I decided to stop playing pregnancy roulette, I went cold turkey. Since then, it's only been me and my silicone friends."

"Cold turkey is a hell of a way to put it."

"Yeah. That's how I think about it."

Brad put his hand over hers. "Maybe we could talk about something else for a bit?"

"Yeah, talking about *anything* else sounds like a good idea."

He looked at his glass. "I definitely need to refresh my drink."

"Me, too."

They walked toward the nearest bar. As they stood quietly in line, Devika surprised herself by putting her free hand in Brad's.

Chapter 15

Everywhere

Fleetwood Mac

*B*reathe, dude. Keep breathing. That absolutely sucked, but I got through it, and Devika didn't run screaming. By the same token, I didn't run screaming at her revelation. I have no idea what this all means, but I think it's progress.

What is she—oh, her hand feels good. Like when she hugged me. I've missed genuine human contact for—for my whole life. Maybe I got contact from Mom when I was very young, but Dad put a stop to anything he considered "unmanly" for as long as I can remember. Feelings were for wimps and girls, and I had to be a man. I guess being *a man meant being emotionally unattached, unable to connect with people, and really fucking lonely. Whatever I am now, and however painful it is, it's much better than being my dad's version of a man.*

Brad enjoyed the feeling of Devika's hand in his. Taking a risk, he adjusted his grip so their fingers intertwined. Brad looked over and grinned at her. Devika grinned back.

They refilled their drinks and wandered back to their still-empty corner of the party. Brad walked up to the window and looked out at the Puget Sound. Somewhere in the darkness beyond the clouds was the majestic Olympic mountain range, their uncaring peaks ancient yet geologically young. He felt like maybe his problems weren't so consequential when considered in the lifespan of a mountain.

Shaking himself out of his reverie, Brad noted Devika was next to him again. They silently watched a ferry slowing as it approached the docks.

"Can I tell you something?" Brad murmured, not wanting to break the spell.

Just as softly, Devika replied, "Sure."

"I like holding your hand. From my earliest memories, I was told showing emotions or gently touching another person was weak and feminine. Holding your hand, or the hug we shared at the party, has made me realize just how stupid that thinking is."

Devika slipped her hand into his. "Both toxic and incredibly stupid. Humans aren't built to be alone. Think about yoga—yoga is all about balance, but sometimes we need another person to balance us out."

"Like having a yoga buddy." Brad smirked stupidly at his joke.

Devika bumped his hip with hers. "Exactly. I know I felt the strength of your—connection when we hugged." She giggled.

Oh no, she definitely felt my hard-on.

"I'm so sorry, Devika."

"Hush, Brad. It's fine. I'm well aware that your dick has a mind of its own."

"I know, but I feel like he ruined a perfect moment between us."

"Oh, he definitely got between us." Devika's shoulders were shaking now. "He made it *hard* to concentrate." Her voice was starting to quiver. "I really wanted to keep hugging you, but something urgently *came* up."

Brad chuckled. "He definitely *pricked* a bad time to show up."

Devika snorted, which set them both to laughing. "I'm just sad you left *half-cocked*."

"Afterward, I needed a *schlong* walk."

"Oh my god, you didn't just say schlong," she exclaimed. "Men are so pre—*dick*—table."

"Hey, I'm just glad you're laughing about this. If you called the cops on me, then I'd end up in a *penal* colony."

"Wow. You had to work for that pun."

Brad nodded. "I did."

Devika looked at him. "Are we done with dick jokes?"

"Yeah, I think so."

She leaned her head against his shoulder. "Good. But don't think we're hugging again any time soon. I don't want you to get *cocky*."

He snorted. "You're so bad."

Laughter is the best medicine, supposedly. If we can laugh after our conversation earlier, then we can probably be friends.

They stood next to each other for a good thirty or so minutes, watching the big ferry dock, offloading people and cars, then loading up for a return trip across the Sound. As they watched the behemoth slowly accelerate, Brad noticed Manny and Nelson in the reflection.

"You know your ex-husband and his boyfriend are watching us, right?"

"I know. They've been there for about ten minutes."

"Do you think they're talking about us?"

"Oh, they are *definitely* talking about us. Fuck 'em. I'm happy right here."

"You are?" Brad was surprised by this revelation.

"Absolutely. I'm lonely, too, Brad. I've missed human contact. Real human contact. It's been such a long time."

"So, we're good?"

"Oh, you're still an asshole." Devika's voice was surprisingly sweet. "But I can't think of anyone else I would want to be here with right now."

Brad chuckled self-effacingly. "I'm not sure how I feel about that, but I can live with it. Thank you, yoga buddy, for helping me balance."

"You're welcome. Now shut up and watch the ferries."

Eventually the party filled up, and their oasis of silence disappeared into the murmur of the crowd. They walked around, mingling with the other guests. Nelson introduced them to the other partners. With the exception of bathroom trips, they were never further than arm's reach.

Ten minutes before midnight, Nelson escorted Brad, Devika, and Manny to the private partners' lounge upstairs.

Showtime.

The four looked down at the rest of the party and the city beyond as the clock ticked toward midnight. Brad and Devika slowly drifted back. Brad silently handed Devika her camera and palmed the jewelry box.

"Ten," the crowd shouted. Devika brought her camera up.

"Nine." She adjusted the focus.

"Eight." Brad carefully opened the jewelry box.

"Seven." Nelson pointed to something.

"Six." Manny looked.

"Five." Nelson whispered something.

"Four." Nelson stepped back.

"Three." Brad handed him the box.

"Two." Nelson knelt, holding up the box.

"One." Manny turned and saw the man he loved. Devika snapped the photo.

"Happy New Year!"

Devika kept taking shot after shot as Manny embraced Nelson, dancing and kissing excitedly. Manny held up his new ring and kissed Nelson long and hard.

Perfect timing, Nelson. They're so in love. Maybe one day I'll have a chance to be just as happy. And not fuck it up this time.

Manny and Nelson finally came up for air. Nelson looked over at the other two. "You didn't have a New Year's kiss."

Brad felt his face coloring. "That's okay. I'm just happy to be here for your moment."

"Same," Devika echoed.

Manny scolded, "You need a New Year's kiss. It's bad luck if you don't."

Nelson echoed him. "Right, you don't want a year of bad luck, do you?"

Devika looked at Brad. "Fine. If it will shut you two up."

Really? Just keep it to a quick friendly kiss.

She walked toward him. He imagined a sultry fire in her eyes but quickly shoved that dream into his subconscious. Devika stood before him, almost as tall as he was. They leaned forward and their lips touched.

Oh my god, her lips are perfect.

Brad pulled back quickly. He laughed nervously. "Bad luck averted. Thank you."

Did I imagine a flash of anger in Devika's eyes?

Chapter 16

Edge of a Broken Heart

Vixen

What the hell, Brad? What was that bullshit kiss? We were having a moment. Hell, we had an entire evening of moments, and then you kissed me like nothing we shared mattered? Nope. I'm out.

Whatever mood was there before was gone. Devika grabbed a ride home soon after. She spent New Year's day stewing. Devika put on a happy face for Manny and Nelson, celebrating with them in the afternoon. Inside, she just felt turmoil. Not even meditation helped.

Brad's a cheater. A serial cheater. Sure, you had a nice evening with him, and maybe you were almost feeling like you could overlook his past and take a risk. That kiss, though. He's clearly not interested. Why risk anything for nothing? I'm not going to do something stupid. What a waste of an evening. At least Manny and Nelson are happy. Which only makes me feel more alone. I'm trying to open myself up to love, and Brad is definitely not worth my time and energy. I just need to stop thinking about him.

Tuesday morning, she stopped by her office for a business card. Dialing the cell number listed, she got voicemail. "Hi, Mike. It's Devika. You asked me out last month, and I'm wondering if you're still interested." She'd run into Mike a few times last year. He was a lawyer in the mayor's office. Handsome, charming, smart, and flirty.

Let's give Mike a shot at love.

Devika's phone rang forty minutes later.

"Hi, Devika. It's Mike. Sorry, I was in a meeting."

"No problem."

"I didn't expect your call, but I'm thrilled to hear from you. Yes, I would love to go out with you."

"That's great—"

"How about dinner on Thursday?"

She giggled. "You're not wasting any time."

"Of course not. Only an idiot wouldn't jump at the opportunity to go out with you." Mike's voice oozed charm and earnestness.

I'm supposed to meet Brad for yoga, but this is a better use of my evening. Mike is right, and Brad is clearly an idiot.

Devika felt calmer, yet she was also excited about her date with Mike. The time seemed to fly as the hour of her date approached. She did see Brad briefly on Wednesday—she was leaving her intermediate class, and he was heading to the beginner class.

"Hey, Brad. I can't go to class with you tomorrow, I have a date."

"A date? Oh. Good for you, yoga buddy."

"Anyway, have a good class." She rushed out without looking back.

See, he's fine. I was just reading too much into things before his awful kiss. Whatever. Tomorrow, maybe Mike will give me a real kiss.

Thursday evening, Devika raced home and put on a black skirt and cream blouse. A silver belt, silver necklace, black cardigan, and low-heeled black pumps completed the outfit. She checked herself in the mirror before leaving.

I look good. Damn good. Classy, a bit sexy, but not too sexy. I want to give just the right impression.

She arrived at the restaurant early, approving the choice. It was an upscale bar and grill, which subtly suggested pricey, but not ostentatious. A text from Mike indicated he was running a few minutes late. Something came up at the office.

Devika was getting a bit frustrated when "a few minutes" became twenty minutes, but her irritation ebbed when Mike pulled up to the valet stand.

Damn, he looks good. His suit is business-like, yet somehow sexy. Maybe he was just freshening up. Mmm, his smile. He looks so cool and relaxed, with just enough swagger.

"Hey, Devika. Sorry I kept you waiting. A last minute thing came up that had a tight deadline. I finished a bit faster than I liked, but I think all parties are satisfied with the outcome." His grin sent electric shocks down her spine.

"No problem. Thanks for texting. I didn't wait long."

"I'm glad. Damn, babe. You look stunning."

Devika smiled blissfully at the compliment. "You're not so bad yourself."

Mike leaned in for a friendly cheek kiss, and then gestured toward the door. "Shall we?"

What the hell is his cologne? It makes me think of sex. Hot, sweaty sex.

The date was fabulous. Mike was a witty conversationalist, and kept Devika entertained throughout. His phone kept buzzing, and at one point, she said, "Do you need to answer your phone?"

"No," he replied smoothly. "Whatever it is isn't as important as you."

He's so hot.

After dinner, Mike walked Devika to the curb. "Are you sure I can't give you a ride home?" he asked.

"No, it's fine. My ride is almost here. Thank you for tonight. Dinner was amazing."

"You're welcome, and it's only because of how amazing you are."

Devika felt the heat in her cheeks. "Can we do this again soon? Saturday perhaps?"

"Ugh. I wish I could. I'm booked all weekend, though. How about next Thursday?"

"I'm not sure I can wait so long, but if I have to, I will."

"I'm so sorry, Devika. I wish I could go on a date with you every single night. I'm not sure how I'll survive without seeing you, either."

"Maybe you just need something to remember me by." Devika leaned toward Mike, lips pursed and eyes blazing.

He moved to meet her, and she felt electricity running from her lips down to her toes. Her nostrils were full of his strange, sexy, heady scent, and her body pulsed in response. She slumped a bit as her car pulled up, ending the moment.

"Goodnight, Mike. Thank you again."

"Goodnight, Devika. It was my pleasure."

At home, Devika skipped meditation and went straight for her collection of vibrators. She slept well that night.

Chapter 17
Teenage Dirtbag
Wheatus

*S*he has a date. We're friends, and I can support her. Devika said she needed to open herself up to love, and I'm glad she's taking this step.

Right, Brad. If you tell yourself this enough, you might even believe your own bullshit.

No, not bullshit. I do believe we're just friends.

And our kiss? You felt it. The untapped passion boiling toward the surface. You know, right before you chickened out and pulled back.

Where has untapped passion gotten me in life? Divorced and alone.

Be honest with yourself, Brad. It wasn't passion that got you here. It was arrogance and fucking stupidity. We coasted through life, either avoiding decisions or making the worst decisions. The closest thing I have to success in my entire life is Sophia, and let's face it, Megan deserves ninety-nine percent of the credit there.

Ugh, I hate myself.

That's part of the problem. Being an asshole for most of the last thirty-three years hasn't exactly set me up for success at redeeming myself. Maybe following some passion might be a welcome change.

It's not like I can go back and change things, especially now that Devika's dating.

Talking to myself isn't helping. It might be time for therapy.

Therapy could help. Talking with anyone could help. Maybe Nelson wants to go to the game tomorrow.

Class wasn't helpful. Brad's inability to focus caused him to lose his balance again and again. By the end, he was a seething ball of frustration. Desperately needing some human interaction, Brad texted Nelson about the Kraken game Thursday night. Nelson responded with interest, but asked Brad to hold off on getting tickets.

At home, Brad petted Cricket, who was enjoying nightly snuggles in his lap. As she made her cat biscuits in preparation for her nap, Brad decided to try something new. It was time to join the modern world and download a dating app. Having no idea what to do, Brad did some research, looking for ratings and reviews. He opted against a site many considered good for finding marriage as well as another more focused on casual hook-ups. He picked one seemingly between those two poles and started a profile.

Cricket was sleeping soundly and getting surprisingly heavy by the time Brad finished. Looking at the time, Brad lifted the startled cat off his lap and made his way toward bed.

At lunchtime on Thursday, Brad had a message from Nelson informing him the game was on for later in the evening and that Nelson had a surprise for him. Furthermore, Brad didn't need to worry about tickets. After reading Nelson's email, Brad was surprised to find he had quite a few matches on the dating app. He spent most of his lunch break checking his matches on the app, which forced him to wolf down his food in the final few minutes before going back to work.

Before I go further, I really need to tighten up my parameters. Let's keep the age range to five years up or down from me and exclude anyone in a relationship. Some of those suggestions were...spicy.

Brad felt better about his dating prospects by the time he reached the arena. He stepped off the bus and went to meet Nelson, who gave him a bear-hug when they met. Brad followed him into the arena, feeling curious about Nelson's surprise. His pulse picked up as Nelson led him toward the arena marked for sky boxes.

No way. This is gonna be awesome! Nelson does work at a wealthy architectural firm. They probably have a box, or he knows someone who does.

Brad was practically giddy when they reached the luxury suite. Nelson showed him in, and Brad got his first look at the ice from the rich person's perspective. It was awesome. They settled in with food and drinks to watch the game.

"How are you, my friend?" Nelson asked companionably.

"I'm great, especially now. How are you? Is engaged life treating you well?"

"Strange. I never thought this would happen for me. I love it, though."

"Dude, I'm happy for you."

"It's not all sunshine and roses, though. Only a handful of people knew he wasn't married to Devika anymore. Manny's company does a lot of business with foreign and conservative clients who take a dim view of his sexuality."

And up until I'm not sure when, I was one of those people. Maybe I'm not an asshole anymore. Eh, let's not get too far out there. Maybe I'm not a complete *asshole anymore. Partial asshole is progress.*

"Is he in trouble?"

"No. At least in the state of Washington, he can't be fired for being gay. That said, a rival construction firm has been trying to poach him for years, and their offer is suddenly looking more attractive by the day."

"So, it's been a mixed blessing for Manny?"

Nelson sighed heavily. "He's rightfully proud of what he's built at his company—literally and figuratively—but Devika and I have been subtly nudging him for years to find a place that is a better fit for him. Speaking of my fiancé's ex-wife—how are things?"

"Well, we were supposed to go to yoga together tonight, but she canceled because she has a date."

Nelson sat upright, exclaiming, "Bloody hell, Brad. How did you fuck that up?"

"Wait, what?"

"Fancy dress event, open bar, romantic atmosphere, plus the side effects of being there for the proposal. I thought something was wrong after that horrible kiss, but I didn't think it was so bad she'd immediately find someone else."

"You were trying to set us up?"

"I bowled that right onto your bat. All you had to do was swing."

"Huh?"

"Cricket. I'll teach you someday. Anyway, Devika's on a date tonight? With who?"

"No clue." Brad added plaintively, "She just said she was going on a date."

"Well? What are you going to do about it?"

"There's nothing I can do. I did get myself on a dating app."

Nelson buried his head in his hands, mumbling to himself. He finally looked at Brad. "I don't know what to say. I guess, are you trying to date to make her jealous?"

"Jealous? Why? We're just friends."

Nelson stammered, trying to find words. Finally, he said, "Brad, you two spent almost two hours holding hands, watching the fucking ferries dock—in the middle of a party. You're not just friends, or at least you weren't right then." He stood up. "Fucking Americans. Give me a minute. I have to tell Manny about this cock-up."

Brad was left watching the players warm up as Nelson talked animatedly on his phone. Nelson eventually came back and sat down. "Manny says you're the dumbest goddamn man he's ever met."

"Oh."

"He also said that even a gay man could have scored."

"Ouch. Come on, man. That's harsh."

Nelson cocked an eyebrow at Brad. "It's also true."

"Look, I'm not trying to score."

"We don't mean sex, Brad, although you'd be an improvement over both her slut phase and the current nun phase."

"You know about...?"

"Of course, we know. It's not like she was particularly discreet at the time. Her taste in men is atrocious."

"All the more reason for her to not date me."

Nelson scowled. "I wasn't speaking of you, Brad."

"Trust me, I'm an asshole. I told her about how I cheated on Megan, multiple times. Including when she was pregnant."

Nelson's scowl softened into a frown. "Cheating on your pregnant wife is pretty bad, my friend." He clapped a hand on Brad's shoulder. "I want you to know something, though. I don't see that man when I look at you."

"Really?"

"Don't get me wrong, you clearly have challenges, but you are striving."

"I'm trying."

"You're doing more than trying, Brad. Tell me honestly, was there a time in your life where you wouldn't have been caught dead watching a hockey game with a gay, Black man?"

Brad blushed. "Yes."

"Was this time recent?"

"Come on—"

Nelson's voice was gentle, even soothing. "Tell me, Brad."

"Yes. Very recent."

Nelson beamed at him. "You see? Not only are we having a nice evening, but you assisted in my engagement."

"True. Since we're being open about this—I consider you a friend, Nelson. I really enjoyed playing a part in your engagement. Manny is a great guy, and you two are a sweet couple. One day I would like to find your kind of love."

"With a man?"

"Uh..."

Nelson cracked up laughing. "You should see your face, Brad. Priceless." He collected himself. "I understand what you mean, and I appreciate it."

"You're killing me, dude."

"Seriously, Brad. Whatever your past, you're a good guy today. Just keep working to be a better person each day." Nelson looked at the ice. "Oh shit, the game's about to start."

They had a good time, watching the game and talking about the strategy. A convincing Kraken win made the evening even better. They enjoyed the view and amenities of the skybox but mutually agreed the game was faster closer to the ice.

Chapter 18
Laid

James

Devika couldn't stop thinking about Mike. About their kiss. Every memory brought heat rushing through her veins. She drifted through Friday like she was in a dream, absently smiling the entire day. Saturday brought the first damper on her mood—Devika had yoga with Brad in the morning.

Going to yoga with Brad makes me feel like I'm cheating on Mike. We're friends, and Brad has made that perfectly clear, but it just feels wrong. We had those intimate moments at the party, which makes seeing him feel icky now. Maybe I'm overreacting. I've only been on one date with Mike. Sure, it was phenomenal, but it's not like we're a couple. When we are, I'm cutting Brad off for good.

As usual, they met a few minutes before class, setting up in their now usual spot in the back corner.

"How was class on Thursday?" Devika asked.

"Oh, I actually ended up going to the Kraken game with Nelson instead. Did you know his firm has a skybox? It was awesome."

"The game or the box?"

"Both. Nelson is a great guy."

"Yes, he is. Plus, I'm sure he loves the company since Manny hates sports."

"Yeah. Nelson said multiple times how happy he was to have someone to watch sports with."

"I bet." Devika nodded.

"He said Manny was relieved not to have to pretend to like them since he can just have Nelson go watch with me instead."

"Sounds like Manny." Devika grinned. "My date was amazing, by the way."

"Right. I meant to ask."

"Mike was the perfect gentleman. Smart and funny. So handsome, too."

"I'm really happy for you."

See, he's being a good friend.

"Thanks, yoga buddy."

"You're welcome. Honestly, you inspired me to put myself out there as well."

"Really? How so?"

"I signed up for one of those dating apps. I have a date tonight."

"Oh...good for you."

And now I feel awkward.

"Yeah, her name is Jenny. She's a single mom, so we have something in common. Sort of."

"What are you going to do?"

"I'm going to try something different from my usual play. There's this Mexican restaurant with a live band and wine-tasting."

Devika cocked an eyebrow. "Have you ever tried Mexican food *or* wine tasting?"

"*Nope.* But it sounds like fun."

The start of class forestalled further discussion. Devika noted how Brad's form was improving, and he seemed fairly relaxed today. She felt unbalanced and out of sorts. She stuck with basic forms today, as more advanced variations were eluding her.

After class, Devika made excuses about something to do and rushed off. Once again, meditation didn't help center her emotions. Manny and Nelson were at a B&B on the other side of the Puget Sound, having a couple's weekend. She tried calling Mike, but he didn't answer.

Loneliness ate at her. Each passing hour gnawed at Devika's psyche. Taking a walk didn't help; neither did reading or watching a movie. Her vibrator helped burn off some pent-up physical needs but left her in even greater emotional anguish.

Sunday morning, she skipped her yoga class, doing a routine at home instead.

Sulking alone isn't helping. I know it's making things worse, but I don't want to go out, either. What is wrong with me? It's like everything started to spiral when I saw Brad. Ugh, I wonder how his date with what's-her-name went. I hope it was a disaster.

I'm not being nice. He's been supportive of me, so I should do the same. It's not like I have any claim to him. I just don't understand. We shared this comfortable and beautiful moment, and now he's suddenly dating some tramp he met on an app. Was our moment too comfortable? Plus, I started dating first. If anything, he should be pissed at me.

Why do I care? We're just yoga friends. Mike is where it's at. I should text him. No, I shouldn't. He said he was busy. Maybe he's doing dumb guy stuff. Oh, I know what I can do.

Devika showered and changed into comfortable-yet-classy loungewear. Something with just enough lace to tease. She took a selfie and sent it to him. His response came an hour or so later. "Damn, babe. I wish I was with you." The loneliness didn't go away, but now at least she was thinking about Thursday.

Chapter 19
Jessie's Girl
Rick Springfield

"Mike was the perfect gentleman. Smart and funny. So handsome, too."

Each word was a dagger in Brad's heart.

I almost canceled on Devika today. I can't get Nelson's words out of my mind. "Two hours holding hands and watching ferries dock. Not just friends."

How did I not realize? Why did I pull back from our kiss? Old Brad would have kissed her lights out. I don't want to be Old Brad anymore, but that doesn't mean New Brad needs to be a different kind of idiot.

Now I'm stuck pretending to be happy for her going out on a date with the perfect man. I'm so damn stupid. Please don't tell me the details of your perfect damn date with Mr. Fucking Perfect. Oh god, I hope she didn't sleep with him.

Right, good job, Brad. Did you tell her about your date tonight to make her jealous? Yeah, I did, but it didn't work. I feel awful for even saying anything. What a dick move.

Brad didn't mind that Devika couldn't stay and chat after class.

Probably running off to see Mr. Perfect. Well, I have Ms. Purrfect at home. Sigh.

He did actually have a nice day with Cricket. She was an excellent reading companion. His lap was toasty warm, and she didn't object when he placed his book over her, so long as he gave her scratchings from time to time. Brad's current read was a history of the 1898 coup in Wilmington, North Carolina. The book was well-researched and written, which made its coverage of the subject matter more disturbing.

There's a reason people try to keep the history of these events buried. The Wilmington Massacre shows how cruel the culture was, but also just how fragile progress is. I think about the horrible things I used to believe and how many others like me still believe them. It isn't hard to see how easily history could repeat itself.

He stayed on the couch, reading with Cricket for hours. Eventually, Brad got up to feed Cricket and prepare for his date. He stuck with his comfortable jeans and flannel look, adding an AC/DC t-shirt underneath.

Brad arrived at the restaurant early, looking at the menu and checking his phone to figure out what everything was. *Tamales* looked like a safe and tasty option. Jenny was a couple of minutes late and apologized.

They sat down and figured out their order. After ordering, they sat in an uncomfortable silence, finally broken by Jenny.

"Okay, I'm just going to say it. You actually look like your profile picture."

"Uh, you do, too. Is that unusual?"

"Oh my god, is this your first time?"

Brad looked around nervously. "Yes. I've never been on a date from an app before."

"Wow. Welcome to the exciting world of dating in the modern era." Jenny took a sip of her margarita. "To answer your question, yes, it is unusual. Honestly, I almost turned you down because your picture was too handsome. The last guy I met who had a picture like yours—let's just say he took a *lot* of creative liberties."

"You look a lot like your picture."

"Thank you. I appreciate the compliment, especially since in between when my picture was taken and now, I got married, had two kids, and got divorced."

Brad was a bit taken aback. "Well, I wouldn't have known it."

"That's kind of you to say. Watch out, Brad. Online dating is cutthroat. Everybody lies about something in their profile."

He chuckled. "I feel like such a noob."

Jenny laughed with him. "Don't worry. You'll get better at it."

I don't know if I want to get better at it.

They chatted idly during dinner and relaxed to listen to the band play. As their evening came toward an end, Jenny said, "Thank you, Brad. I haven't done anything like this so far, and I had fun."

"Me, too. Jenny, I'm not sure how to say this—"

"It's okay, Brad. I can see it in your eyes."

"And you're okay?"

"You seem like a nice enough guy, but there's no long-term chemistry here. We can just call it a night now, if you want."

Brad noted a slight pause before those last three words.

Was she extending an invitation, or just catching a breath?

"Thank you for a lovely evening, Jenny."

"You're welcome. Goodnight." She darted in for a quick peck on the cheek before turning for her minivan.

Brad stood there for a bit, rubbing his cheek in bewilderment.

Chapter 20

Tubthumping

Chumbawamba

Devika stood in her closet after work on Thursday, mulling her options. Her first date with Mike had been incredible, and she felt she needed to up her game for date number two.

My skirt needs to be a bit shorter, and my heels need to be a bit higher than last time. Not too much. I don't want him to think I'm easy. Not that it matters tonight anyway, I wouldn't want our first time to be during my period.

I wonder if Brad is going out tonight. When I saw him on Sunday, he said he couldn't chat because he was meeting Michelle at the

Chihuly Garden. Then he canceled on me for Tuesday because he had a date with Jasmine. Three dates with three different women in four days. I guess I can't judge—I had my slut phase after my divorce. He really seemed like he didn't want to do the same thing. What did he say? Something about the next woman he slept with would be someone he felt he could introduce his daughter to. Close enough.

Why am I thinking about Brad screwing around anyway? I've got Mike to look forward to. That man knows how to kiss. Smart, sexy, didn't cheat on his wife multiple times. Definitely a huge upgrade over Brad.

Feeling lighter, almost giddy, Devika carefully chose her outfit. On her way to meet Mike, he texted her to apologize because he would be a few minutes late. Once at her destination, Devika ducked into a nearby Starbucks to keep warm. Mike was only about fifteen minutes late, and Devika walked quickly across the street to meet him once he arrived.

"Babe, I am so sorry I'm late. When the wife of a city councilman knocks on your door and says she needs something taken care of right now, I had to get right on it. I hope you weren't waiting too long."

That's understandable. He's busy, and being a lawyer in the mayor's office means juggling a lot.

"I dunno. You'll have to work hard to make it up to me." Devika knew she had a stupid grin on her face, but she didn't care. She cared even less when Mike leaned in to give her a deep, toe-curling kiss.

He's wearing his sexy cologne again. Actually, it's slightly different from what I remember. It still makes me incredibly horny. Why does my period have to be happening right now?

"All right." She pushed him back coyly. "But the kiss only partially makes up for it."

Mike grinned right back at her. "Oh, what a burden it shall be to make amends."

They laughed as they walked together to the entrance of a jazz club. Devika looked around as they were led to their table.

The lighting here is perfect. Each table is its own intimate space. It's as if we are totally alone, even though it's a crowded room. Mike is such a romantic.

"How was your day, babe?"

"Busy. There's a lot of preparation for the storm tomorrow, so I was out and about taking lots of photos of what was going on."

"Do you think it will be bad?"

"Not in the main part of the city. Outlying areas could be ugly, though."

"I was thinking the same thing."

"This might be a good opportunity for us to spend a quiet weekend in."

Mike shook his head sadly. "I'm really sorry. As amazing as a warm, cozy weekend with you sounds, the mayor needs an emergency team ready just in case."

"You're a lawyer, Mike. Inclement weather response sounds a bit out of your area."

"You'd be amazed how many legal questions can come up during a major emergency."

"Oh." Devika tried to hide her disappointment. "That makes sense. Maybe it won't be so bad, and we can spend some time together."

Like Sunday, when my period will be mostly over.

"We'll see. You are amazing, and I would spend every minute with you if I could."

Mike held her hand and turned to listen to the pianist. Once the song was done, he said, "It could be worse. Apparently, Portland is probably going to get hammered."

Portland. Wasn't there something in Portland this weekend? Right, Brad was going down to see his daughter. Well, I guess he'll just have to stay here and hook up with more random women.

Devika brought her attention back to Mike. He lifted her hand to his lips, gazing softly into her eyes. She could feel her insides melting as his lips grazed her knuckles.

Mike raised his glass in a silent toast, and she followed suit. They turned back to the pianist as he started a new song. Devika absently sipped her wine, enjoying the music and Mike's silent company.

Two hours later, Devika was feeling woozy. *I can't remember refilling my wine glass, but somehow it was always full. Better lean into Mike and make it seem like I'm snuggly, because I don't think I can walk straight. Tonight, I'm definitely letting him drive me home.*

The streets passed in a blurry canvas of colored lights and deep shadows. Devika stared out the window of Mike's car, seeing everything and nothing at the same time. Finally, she recognized her building. She was home. Her head wobbled as she turned toward Mike.

He kissed her gently at first. The kiss grew more frantic as their passion increased.

"Should I make sure you get in bed okay?"

Mmm, bed. And Mike. Mike in my bed. With me. That's perfect. Shit! *My period—I'm a bloody mess down there.*

"Mike, I really want to, but I can't tonight. My friend is visiting."

He looked confused. "Your friend?"

Devika nodded, her movements more pronounced than normal. "My friend who visits every month. You know."

"Ugh, your friend." Mike grimaced. "You're right, I better let you go then."

"Thank you, Mike, for a wonderful evening."

Was it? I can't remember. Holy shit, I am wasted. How much wine did I drink? I hope I didn't embarrass myself.

"Goodnight, babe."

Devika staggered a bit as she exited his car. She walked toward the door with deliberate care, trying very hard not to sway. Her keys didn't want to stay in her hand, but she eventually got the lock to work. Devika turned to wave, but couldn't see Mike. She staggered to her apartment and flopped wearily onto the bed.

Chapter 21
Purple Rain
Prince

Postponed due to inclement weather. Brad read the notification again and cursed. He had been following the weather all week and wasn't surprised, but still disappointed. Brad reached for his phone and called Megan.

"Hey, Brad. I guess you saw."

"Yeah."

"I'm sorry. Sophia was looking forward to seeing you and going to watch roller derby with you."

"I was looking forward to seeing her, too. Are you all free in two weeks for the rescheduled games?"

"We should be."

Brad immediately felt better. "I'm excited to watch roller derby with Sophia again. Her boot camp is next weekend, right?"

"It is. Sophia and her new friend Ruby are over the moon about it."

"Please tell me how it goes."

"I will."

"How are you and Tasha doing?"

"Good. Really good." He could hear the contented smile in her voice.

"I hear the ice could be really bad in Portland. Are you ready?"

Megan sighed. "Hopefully. We're as ready as we can be."

"Tell me if you need anything, okay?"

"We're fine, Brad."

She's pissed at me now. Be better, Brad.

"I'm sorry, Megan. I overstepped."

She sighed. "No. You're fine. Thank you for your offer, and I'll keep you in mind. I still have a lot of feelings to process about you, and sometimes I can be touchy."

"I understand. I've got a lot of feelings to process about you, too. And about me."

"Hmm?"

"Remember Nelson? We've been to a couple hockey games together, and next Friday, he invited me over to watch cricket—cricket the sport, not Cricket my cat."

"That's good. Speaking of…how's your yoga buddy?"

"I think I screwed up beyond salvaging."

"Uh-oh. How—actually, no. I'm not going to talk about your love life with you. That's just too weird, and I know it's going to set me off."

"Fair. Sorry, Megan." He paused to take a deep breath. "It probably won't make you feel better, but I'm seeing a therapist on Tuesday."

"A therapist? For what?"

"Uh, everything I guess. I have a lot of shit to work on."

Megan snorted. "You're putting it mildly." She paused. "Sorry, even if it's true, I shouldn't have put you down. Just so you know, it does make me feel better to know you're seeing a therapist. You didn't mention anything last time. How did you get an appointment this soon?"

"I got super lucky with a cancellation."

"Good for you, Brad."

"Thanks, Megan. One last thing."

"Yeah?"

"I'm taking the train down in two weeks for roller derby, weather permitting. Do you think you could pick me up at the station or some other place?"

Brad assumed the subsequent silence was Megan thinking. "I can get you. Maybe the four of us can have dinner or something."

"I'd love to have dinner." He tried to keep the welling tears out of his voice. "I won't keep you. Please give Sophia my love and say hi to Tasha for me."

"I will. Thanks for calling, Brad."

"Thank you for answering, Megan. Bye for now." They ended the call.

I miss you, Megan. You and Sophia both. More than anything, I miss what could have been if I hadn't been such a dick.

Brad sent everyone home early on Friday to avoid the potential nasty weather, staying alone to close up. Once home, he made himself a grilled cheese sandwich and fed Cricket. He played with her a bit before they got down to serious snuggling. Brad tried to read, but he couldn't focus. Instead, he looked at potential matches on the dating site. Michelle definitely wanted a second date, but he got a weird vibe off of her.

Old Brad definitely would have gone on a second date with Michelle. I'm pretty sure she wants to sleep with me, especially given some of her comments in the glass museum. New Brad made a promise, though, and New Brad keeps his promises. Then there's Jasmine. I want to ask her out for a second date, but I think it's because she looks like Devika and not because I like her. Again, not what New Brad should do.

Devika. I feel like we're avoiding each other. I'm just as complicit in our avoidance as she is. She's probably spending the stormy weekend in Mr. Perfect's arms. Meanwhile, I'm home alone with a cat. A cute and fuzzy cat. Aw, she snored.

I need to stop thinking about her. *So, the next best option is go out with strangers who probably lied on their profile to see if maybe we connect. Oh god, that sounds awful just saying it to myself. Also, I'm getting worried about the number of conversations I'm having with myself.*

Brad woke up on Saturday to a text from Megan informing him they were okay. He scrolled through reports of massive power outages and a solid coating of ice over Portland before getting out of bed. After feeding Cricket and himself, he scheduled a date later in the day with Isabella.

He dressed warmly and met Isabella at the Olympic Sculpture Park. She was a cute brunette who looked like her profile picture.

Probably a good sign.

"Hi, I'm Brad."

"Isabella. Good to meet you. This is insane, you know that, right?"

"A walk along the waterfront followed by ice cream? I think it's a perfect date."

She laughed. "Yeah, for July."

"Exactly. I thought it might be fun to recreate the spirit of summer in January."

She shook her head. "Crazy, but I'm game to try it. I'll warn you, I might need some hot chocolate to go with my ice cream."

"Good thinking." He beamed at her. "Shall we?" Brad crooked his arm, and Isabella took it, huddling to keep him between her and the frigid wind.

Later, as they nursed their hot chocolates, Isabella stated, "That was, without question, the worst date idea of all time." She followed her statement up with a laugh. "But it was bold and unexpected. I appreciate the creativity." Isabella took a sip of her drink and peered at Brad over the rim. "Maybe we could have another date, preferably warm and indoors. You know, like a restaurant."

Brad chuckled. "I'd like a do-over."

"Great. I'll pick the restaurant." She grinned flirtatiously. "Just to be safe."

They agreed on the following Saturday for a second date, then Isabella had to go as she needed to change for another date that evening. Brad bade her good luck and they parted ways.

It seems strange to tell a woman I just had a date with "good luck" on her date with another guy—girl—person—right after mine. I can't object though, as I have a first date with Yessica tomorrow. We're meeting for late morning coffee, so I'll have to do an afternoon yoga class, which means I won't see Devika, which is probably for the best.

Why am I such a coward?

Chapter 22

Flirtin' With Disaster

Molly Hatchet

Devika was crushed when her boss assigned her to cover aftereffects of the storm all weekend. The overtime was poor compensation for missing out on the chance to snuggle with Mike. She felt his absence the most on Sunday as her flow dissipated, and she contemplated the sex they could have been having.

At least he didn't seem to be put off by my drunken state on Thursday. I'm mortified that I drank so much.

He called her Sunday afternoon, and she immediately picked up. "Mike, I've been missing you."

"Me too, babe. This weekend has been awful. I got called into the office today. I'm driving in right now."

"Mmm, I could meet you there," Devika purred.

"I like your naughtiness. Sadly, I'll be stuck deep into some sticky issues. As much as I'm dying to see you, it's not a good idea."

"Oh, poo," she pouted.

"Babe, I need to see you soon. Maybe Thursday again?"

"What about Friday?"

"Friday would be—oh, damn. I can't. My buddy Sean is in town all weekend, and I promised to spend time with him."

"I can come along. You can show me off to your friend."

Wow, I sound fucking desperate.

"I like your thinking, because he would be so jealous. It's just—this thing between us is so new. I feel selfish. Like I want to keep you all for myself, at least for right now. But when we're ready, babe, I'm going to shout it from the rooftops."

I hate it, but he's worth waiting for.

"Yeah, so Thursday. What are you thinking? You should totally pick our next date, because I know it will be perfect."

"Aw, you're so sweet. I'm not sure how I could top our first two dates, though."

"I know you can. You're smart, beautiful, and fun, so whatever you decide will surely put my date ideas to shame."

"Mike, I have an idea."

"I can't wait to hear it."

"You could come over to my place, and I'll fix you dinner. I hope I don't sound immodest, but I've been told I'm an excellent cook."

"Sounds perfect. Will there be wine and candles?"

"Of course. I'll knock your socks off."

And the rest of your clothes.

"It's a date. You're the best, babe. Okay, I gotta go. Talk soon."

"All right, I can't wait, Mike."

Monday and Tuesday blew by in a blur. Wednesday dawned cold, both outside and in Devika's mind.

Tomorrow is the big day. I'm going to cook him the best damn dinner I've ever made, but what happens next? I definitely want sex, but it's day ten of my cycle. Sunday would have been so much better, as I would have been totally safe. To have our first time totally bare would have been perfect. Day ten, though. I mean, it's probably low risk, but it's still risky. I can ask him to use a condom, but what if he doesn't want to? I mean, of course he doesn't want to. There's other options for sex with no risk—not many men would turn down anal, but anal isn't my favorite.

I've got time to think about it. I'll figure out something.

Devika did think about it—a lot. It consumed her every waking hour. She kept going back and forth in her mind. By Thursday evening, she felt frazzled. Putting on a brave face, she drowned her anxiety in cooking. She had *tandoori* chicken and *aloo saag* ready by the time Mike arrived. As usual, he was a few minutes late, but he made sure to kiss her thoroughly to make up for it.

He has his sexy cologne on again. Holy shit, I am wet from his smell, and the kiss.

"Welcome to my home, Mike. Make yourself comfortable."

She watched him survey her apartment. The lights were turned down, and candles were already burning at the table.

"It smells amazing, babe."

"Just wait until you taste it."

And then taste me. Damn. I'm so nervous to ask him about using a condom. I shouldn't be so nervous. We're adults. What if he says no?

Devika continued, "I'm making the *naan* now. It won't be long."

"I can't wait." Mike sat down, scrolling through his phone while Devika finished the *naan*.

"Mike, can you give me a hand?"

"Sure." He walked over and she handed him two hot mitts and the *tandoori* chicken. He shuttled the *aloo saag* and the rice over as well.

As Mike put the last dish on the table, Devika said, "Hey, if you need to wash up, the bathroom is to the left."

"Good call, babe."

He went into the bathroom. She could hear the water going when his phone buzzed on the counter next to her. Devika looked over and saw the preview of a series of text messages on his screen.

> Becca: *I'm sorry you have to work late again, sweetie.*

> *I hope you get home soon.*

> *I'm wearing something naughty for you.*

> *You were such an animal when you came home last Thursday.*

> *I'm hoping for an encore.*

Devika stared at the screen in shock. She whispered to herself, "What the fuck?"

Mike walked out of the bathroom. "Hey, babe. Let's eat."

Devika snatched up his phone, hurling it at him. She screamed, "Get the fuck out of my apartment, you worthless pile of shit!"

He stared at her in shock.

"Go get your encore from Becca. She's wearing something naughty for you."

"Look, babe. It's not what you think. She's this crazy bitch who's been stalking me."

"Oh, fuck you, Mike. Get the fuck out of here now!" She snatched the knife sitting by the sink, the blade quivering in her grip.

"All right. I'm going. No need to get nasty."

Devika was practically spitting with rage. "We're nowhere near nasty yet, but you'll find out just how nasty I can get if you aren't out of my damn door in the next five seconds."

As the door slammed shut behind Mike, Devika raced over and locked it. She turned around, her back pressed against the door as she slid down to the floor. Devika wrapped her arms around her knees and rocked back and forth, weeping copiously.

Chapter 23

You Oughta Know

Alanis Morissette

Devika went in to work early on Friday with a mission in her mind. She told her boss she needed the day off but had to take care of a few things first. He looked confused, but let her get on with what she was doing. Devika pulled the drunken selfie from eight days ago off her phone and converted it into an eight by ten hard copy photo. Next, she called an acquaintance in the mayor's office and got the phone number of Mike's personal assistant. Devika then called Mike's assistant and made up a story about how Mike asked her to drop off some photos with someone named Becca, but

Mike had gotten the contact information wrong. She asked Mike's assistant to give her the correct contact information for Becca.

With Becca's work address in hand, Devika set off on the next stage of her revenge tour. Sitting in the back of a cab in the harsh light of day, she thought back to her first two dates with Mike.

There was something about his scent. It wasn't cologne, or if it was, it was mixed with something else. If I had to guess, he had another woman's juices on him. Holy shit. The arrogant bastard was flaunting just having sex before our date.

What did he say the first time? Something came up and they reached a mutual settlement or some bullshit. The fucking asshole was late because he was screwing another woman minutes before our date. Oh, shit. The second time. He said something about a city councilman's wife wanting something, and he gave it to her. Oh my god, if I can figure out whose wife he's screwing, then I can hang this bastard out to dry.

The cab pulled up to a modern, high-rise office building. Devika paid the cabbie and got out, walking swiftly toward the glass doors. Inside, there was a large security desk in the atrium, preventing access to the upper floors.

This is a stupid plan, but it's the best I've got right now.

Devika strode confidently up to the desk, a legal envelope in hand.

"I have a delivery for Rebecca Hartford."

"Credentials, please."

"Uh, I'm not with a service. I work for the city of Seattle." She showed her ID badge. "My boss sent me over here to deliver these photos."

"Uh-huh." The guard looked dubious. "Give me a minute." He reached for a phone and then stopped. He called out to a middle-aged woman approaching the security gates. "Ms. Huntsman, do you know Ms. Hartford?"

"Yes, she's one of my associates. Why?"

"This lady has some photos from the city of Seattle for Ms. Hartford."

The woman's eyes narrowed. "Who sent you?"

Time to roll the dice.

"Mike Thompson sent me. A special package just for Ms. Hartford."

Her eyes narrowed further. "Interesting." She turned to the guard. "Chuck, please issue a visitor pass for Miss...?"

"Kumar. Devika Kumar."

Way to go, super spy. Using your actual name.

Pass in hand, Devika followed Ms. Huntsman to the elevators. When the doors opened, they entered, and Ms. Huntsman tapped one of the top buttons on the display.

"Now, Ms. Kumar. What are you actually doing?"

"This is just for Becca. Ms. Hartford."

"Are you a private investigator?"

"Uh..."

"No. Mike Thompson has a reputation. Let me guess, you have a photo of him with a woman." She studied Devika's face. "A photo with you..."

"I swear I didn't know, but Becca deserves to know."

"So, you're going to ruin her life because you're upset?"

"It's not just me. Before each of our dates, I think he had sex with other women, including a city councilman's wife."

The woman's eyebrows arched at her last piece of information. "Do you have proof?"

Devika looked down. "No."

The doors opened, and she followed the older woman into the lobby of a law firm.

"Tell me what you do have," she whispered.

Devika quietly said, "He dated me. I have proof of our two dates. He hinted at sexual affairs, but I was too blinded to pick up on it at the time. Also, he smelled like—he smelled like pussy. I think he was using his lover's juices as cologne."

"Bold choice." Ms. Huntsman lapsed into thought, clearly considering what to do. "All right. Follow me, Ms. Kumar."

Devika trailed the woman into a small conference room. "Close those blinds and take a seat, Ms. Kumar." She left, closing the door behind her. Devika did as instructed, nervously fingering the envelope in her hands.

After an interminable wait, the door opened, and a young blond woman entered. "Ms. Kumar? I was told you have something for me."

Do I shake her hand or something? This is awkward. Well, it's about to get much *more awkward.*

Devika stood, extending a hand. "You must be Becca." The woman nodded. "I'm not really sure how to say this..."

"Say what? Is something wrong with Mike?"

His name burned in Devika's ears, fueling the embers of her rage into a roaring conflagration. "Yes, there's something wrong with Mike, all right. Last night, when he told you he was working late, he was actually in my apartment for a dinner date."

Devika watched the color drain from Becca's face with each word. "I saw your texts. How you were wearing something naughty. How he was an animal when he came home the previous Thursday. Want to know why he was an animal last Thursday night?" Devika opened the envelope, displaying the drunken selfie of her and Mike with their lips locked together. "Because I didn't sleep with him before he went home to you."

The poor woman collapsed in a chair, her face a mask of horror. Becca put her hands to her mouth, and that's when Devika saw the diamond on her left ring finger.

"I'm so sorry, Becca. I swear I never slept with him. On each of our dates, he arrived late, smelling of another woman's scent. I didn't recognize it at the time, but I realized it later."

"Please go. Just go."

Standing, Devika left the photo and walked out. She closed the door behind her, leaving Becca sobbing at the table. Ms. Huntsman was waiting outside. She asked sternly, "It didn't feel as good as you thought it would, did it?"

Devika shook her head silently.

"Don't worry. I will take good care of Ms. Hartford." The older woman grinned wickedly. "And I'll make sure to take care of Mr. Thompson as well."

I never want to be on this woman's bad side.

"Thank you. I'm sorry. For everything."

Devika rode the elevator down alone. She returned the badge at the security desk and walked out into the cold, damp Seattle air. It matched her mood perfectly.

Chapter 24
I Will Survive
Gloria Gaynor

Devika's apartment was cold and lonely, but the faint scent of spices lingered in the air, reminding her of the shitshow that was the last twenty-four hours of her life. She contemplated throwing out the food from last night, but couldn't bring herself to waste it. Turning away from the kitchen, Devika threw herself on the couch, covered herself in a blanket, and cried until she slept. She woke after night had fallen.

I can't be here alone anymore. I need to see someone—talk to some-one.

Devika changed clothes and headed out, arriving soon after at Nelson's condo. She buzzed, and Manny answered, letting her in. As usual, she opened their door without knocking to find Nelson walking toward the door. "Was that the pizza guy who just buzzed?" Nelson shouted.

Manny answered, "No, it was—" He didn't bother to finish the sentence as both men could see it was her.

"Hi, guys." Devika's voice hitched, and she pawed at a tear descending her cheek. "I'm sorry to come over unannounced."

They clearly saw her distress and descended upon her with hugs. Devika felt better, wrapped in the love of Manny and Nelson. Her momentary good feeling came to a crashing halt when she heard more footsteps. She looked up over Manny's shoulder to see Brad round the corner from the living room.

"What the hell is that cheating bastard doing here?" Devika shrieked. Her knees gave out, and Manny and Nelson struggled to keep her from falling. "I can't be around him right now. I can't." She began sobbing and shaking.

Nelson started to stammer a response, but Brad cut him off. "No problem. I'll get my coat and leave. We'll do this some other time."

Brad was long gone before Devika could mostly compose herself. "I'm sorry. He's a cheater, and I can't be around cheaters right now."

They both squeezed her hands before Manny asked, "Do you want to tell us what happened?"

"I don't want to. It's humiliating, and it hurts so much."

"You don't have to tell us anything you don't want to. We can just hug you in silence."

"Thank you. You should know. Plus, I feel like my whole world has fallen apart, and you two are the only ones I trust right now." Devika took a deep, shuddering breath. "I found out Mike was cheating on me."

Manny and Nelson simultaneously said, "Devika, I'm so sorry."

"Actually, no. That's not true. Mike was cheating on his fiancée with me. And probably at least two other women."

Manny hugged her close while Nelson stood up, clenching his fists angrily. "Bugger that arsehole. You're good to be done with him."

Manny added, "You can tell us as much or as little as you want. We're here for you either way. We'll take care of you."

Devika told them everything, from Mike's flirting last year, her asking him out, their dates—all the way up through revealing his cheating to Becca. Telling this tale took time, as she cried often. They took breaks to eat pizza when Devika felt too emotionally raw to continue.

At the end, Devika looked at Manny and said, "This is all your fault. You know that?" She kept her tone light, and a tiny hint of a smile graced her lips.

"How is this my fault?" Manny spluttered.

"You made me promise to be open to love, and I was. Look where it got me." She felt brittle, but the catharsis of telling her sordid tale was helping.

"I—"

Nelson interrupted. "Manny. If you pop off with some trite saying about how it's better to love and lose, then I shall make you sleep in the guest room."

"Hmph. I stick by it. Just because Mike is an asshole doesn't mean all men are."

"The ones I find are."

"Is that why you wanted Brad out of here?"

Devika suddenly remembered how he'd left in a hurry. "Oh my god, it was so rude of me to have you kick out a guest."

Nelson shook his head. "Technically, we didn't kick him out. He voluntarily offered to leave. Did Brad do something to hurt you?"

"You mean besides getting me all worked up and then giving me the kind of shitty kiss you might give to a leper?" She felt the tears welling again. "He fucking friend-zoned me, and then he's been a shitty friend. Anyway, I want nothing to do with him. Once a liar, always a liar."

Manny gave her a concerned look. "What has he lied about to you?"

Devika shook her head angrily, remembering Brad's words. "He told me about a promise he made to his ex-wife's girlfriend of all people. He swore that the next woman he slept with would be someone he would be willing to introduce to his daughter." She took a deep, calming breath. "And now the lying man-whore is sleeping with half of Seattle."

Manny and Nelson exchanged confused looks.

"What?" Devika snapped at them.

Nelson turned his bewildered gaze on her. "Have you actually talked with Brad lately?"

"No. Why should I?"

"I think you both are making rather large assumptions about each other."

"What's that supposed to mean?" Devika demanded petulantly.

"Nelson is trying to say that you and Brad are not communicating and instead are filling the communication void with your imaginations."

"What do you two care about Brad anyway?"

I feel myself getting defensive and hurt every time they open their mouths. It's not their fault. They want to help, and I'm wounded and lashing out.

"Guys. Forget I said anything. Let's just talk about something else. Literally anything else. Please. I love you two, and I'm sorry I'm being a bitch."

Manny and Nelson gave her hugs and reassured her that her feelings were valid and expected given the pain and trauma of the last couple of days. They promised they didn't take offense. Nelson ended with, "On to other subjects. Devika, would you like to watch cricket with me?" Manny groaned miserably at the suggestion.

Chapter 25
Changes

Black Sabbath

Brad hurried out of the condo, deliberately not looking at Devika. He wasn't sure why she was upset, but he suspected Mr. Perfect turned out not to be so perfect after all.

I can't really feel happy that Mike turned out to be an asshole because I hate seeing Devika in such pain. She called me a cheating bastard—which is true—so it seems likely Mike cheated on her. No matter what, Devika didn't deserve whatever Mike did, just like Megan didn't deserve what I did to her.

Now the question is: what next? I should probably give her space. At the same time, I feel like I should support her. Maybe the best support is giving her space, but I don't know.

Side note: telepathy would be a cool superpower, although probably a relationship killer.

Okay, back to Devika. Smile and keep my distance, I guess. I could have been a better friend these past couple of weeks, but it hurt so much to see her—knowing she was with someone else.

Avoiding her was selfish of me. Speaking of selfishness, I hope the fallout from this Mike disaster doesn't mean I have to stop being friends with Nelson. I was kinda looking forward to figuring out the rules of cricket tonight.

At home, Brad resumed his nightly ritual of reading with Cricket napping in his lap. The tiny cat seemed to love this, and Brad faithfully carved out time every evening for her. He even fell asleep a few nights with her in his lap. After his abrupt exit from Manny and Nelson's place, Brad especially enjoyed his special time with Cricket. Her deep purrs helped soothe his anxiety, and he made sure to reward her with soft petting.

He read for a while once Cricket fell asleep, interrupted only by a small—yet vilely potent—cat fart. Brad woke up Saturday morning, still on the couch. His back was aching and his legs were stiff and sore from the strange position they had worked themselves into during the night to accommodate the cat sleeping between his knees.

Morning yoga helped ease his aches and stiffness. He hoped to see Devika there but wasn't surprised at her absence. Back home, he did some journaling. Brad still felt odd about writing his feelings down;

however, his therapist had suggested it, and he wasn't about to turn away ideas on ways to improve himself. After lunch, he set his book on the couch and meditated. Cricket took this as an invitation for more lap time, so when Brad finished meditating, he was relieved his book was close at hand.

I'm learning how to live with a cat. A very needy and affectionate cat.

Eventually, Brad had to kick Cricket off his lap. He showered and got dressed for his second date with Isabella. She picked a nice Thai restaurant for them, and he wanted to look good. Brad eschewed his typical flannel for a dress shirt. He briefly considered a tie, but opted for a vest instead. The jeans were non-negotiable, though. Satisfied that he looked presentable, Brad set out. He arrived about ten minutes early, and Isabella was a couple of minutes late.

"Sorry I'm late," she said.

Brad smiled. "Two minutes is on time. Also, hi, and you look pretty."

"Hi, and thank you."

"Did I overstep? When I said you look pretty?"

Isabella snickered. "Yes, a little. But I enjoy hearing someone tell me I'm pretty."

"Whew. I didn't want to be too forward. I'm still figuring out the rules of dating."

She paused to consider this. "Well, rule number one: don't go on a summer date in January." She grinned impishly. "That's a good start."

Brad bowed his head. "Yeah, sorry."

"Hey, I'm teasing you. It was my most unique date yet."

"By unique, you mean awful."

"Oh, trust me. I've had much worse. Honestly, I appreciate you trying something different."

"Thanks. Now, let's go try some Thai food." Brad held the door for Isabella, who flitted through quickly. He followed, savoring the warmth after the chilly Seattle evening. Brad decided on the *Pad See Ew,* as it seemed not too spicy. He was warming up to spices but still cautious.

"How was your week? You're a controller for the transportation department, right?"

"Comptroller."

"Right. I was close," Brad said hopefully.

"Not bad, actually." Isabella talked about her week, and Brad nodded along, posing questions to keep the conversation going. It was a struggle for him, as his thoughts kept drifting to Devika. He forced himself to pay attention to Isabella, but his thoughts proved slippery.

"How was learning about cricket?" she asked, bringing the conversation back to him.

"She's such a good cat." He caught the puzzled look on her face. "You meant learning about *cricket.* I can't believe you remembered me mentioning that."

Isabella smiled patiently at him.

"It didn't happen. A friend of Nelson's was having a crisis, so I left to give them space."

"That was nice of you. So, you'll reschedule?"

"Yeah. I hope so."

Isabella gave Brad a quizzical look. "What's going on with you? You seem different."

He tried to laugh it off. "You mean, not like a walking popsicle?"

"Well, yes, but not just being Frosty the Snowman. You're trying too hard."

"What do you mean?"

"Most guys, their eyes glaze over when I talk about work. You don't. Last time, you were fully engaged when I talked shop, which I appreciated. This time...it's like you've been forcing yourself to pay attention. Am I making sense?"

"I'm sorry, Isabella. Nelson's friend in crisis—her name is Devika, and a few weeks ago, I thought we might have had something going. Then, on New Years, we kissed, and I gave her a quick friend kiss, and two days later she started dating another guy. I think they broke up, which was why she was at Nelson's place crying. Whew, I'm sorry for dumping on you."

"First, just let me say I appreciate how you were trying so hard to focus on me. Second, it seems like maybe you want to be more than friends with Devika, but you screwed up."

"You seem strangely calm about this."

"It's like everyone says—online dating is a numbers game. A lot of them don't work out, but if you have enough, then you'll find someone who works for you."

Brad looked at Isabella quizzically. "That sounds awful, but it makes sense."

She nodded in agreement. "Full disclosure, I've been on a few dates with another guy, and we're talking seriously about being exclusive. I did want one more date with you, just to see if there was a spark, because our first date..." Isabella rocked back in her chair, chuckling. "Our first one was a doozy. I do like you, Brad. A couple of months ago, figuring out you were hung up on someone else would have hurt. Now, I'm in a different place."

Online dating hurts my head. Probably my heart, too.

"Honestly, you might have dodged a bullet," Brad said. "I'm still working through a lot of stuff from my divorce. The journey of personal growth appears to be a long one."

"You might be right." Isabella tapped her fingers on her lips. "What's the deal with you and this Devika chick? How did you meet?"

"You really want to know?" Brad felt dumbfounded.

"Sure, why not? I'm feeling confident and empowered about where I'm at, relationship-wise, and I'm sure neither of us want to spend the next hour talking about finances and banking, so let's go. I want to hear the sordid tale of Brad and Devika."

Brad shook his head. "All right, here goes..." He laid out the whole story from their first meeting at the yoga studio until now. Brad considered shading the truth at points, but figured he'd likely never see Isabella again, so he might as well be honest.

The recitation took them through the *satay*, and then their entrees. Once Brad reached the point in the story where he left Manny and Nelson's, they both paused to process.

"All right," Isabella said. "You might be right about me dodging a bullet. Then again, maybe not. Being honest about your past and your mistakes is an important step in changing your behavior. Unless you're an incredible actor, you seem genuinely remorseful. Contrition counts for something."

"Thanks," Brad responded ruefully. "You know how some people say you can't love someone else if you don't love yourself? Well, I'm having a hard time liking myself these days."

"So I see. You did some really shitty things. Forgiving yourself can't be easy."

"Tell me about it."

"Look, Brad. It's probably not my place to say this, but if you are serious about becoming the person your daughter sees you as, then you're going to have to *believe* in your ability to improve."

He nodded. "Makes sense."

Isabella smiled gently. "Your future is in front of you. Never forget your past, and never forget how you feel now, but don't let those memories keep you from moving forward."

Brad chuckled. "Have you ever considered being a therapist?"

"Briefly, but I didn't want to go back to school again. I spent a lot of time in therapy working on my own shit. You're getting the distilled wisdom of my journey."

"Thank you. I appreciate it."

"You're welcome. I hate to be the bearer of bad news, though—I'm still not sure what you should do about Devika."

"Oh." Brad frowned. "I figure what I need to do is give her space, but somehow show her I support her. Now I have to figure out how."

"Is she worth it?"

He didn't hesitate with his answer. "Absolutely."

"Then I hope you figure it out."

"Damn, I was hoping you'd say that you were sure I would."

Isabella laughed, sounding much like the bells in her name. "I don't want to give you false hope. People are unpredictable. I'm sure you will do your best. If Devika is open to your support, then you have a chance."

Brad sighed. "I'll do my best for sure."

Chapter 26

Nobody's Fool

Cinderella

Devika saw *him* again on Sunday morning. She knew it was a risk, but her body and mind craved the rhythms of yoga. He was coming out of the beginner class, sweaty and flushed. Their eyes met, and he gave her a slight smile and a small wave. "Hey, yoga buddy. Have a good class."

She froze in place, fighting the urge to run. He stepped sideways, leaving plenty of space between them. Devika kept her eyes on him as he gingerly kept his distance. Once he was past her, she let out a breath she hadn't realized she was holding. Moving forward again, she walked into class and laid down her mat.

The instructor brought the class together, and Devika lost herself in the progression of poses. The feel of her body moving helped her mind and spirit rise from the depths of depression. "Namaste," she said with the rest of the class. Standing, she felt better than she had in days. The pain wasn't gone, but it was manageable again.

Brad didn't deserve what I said or how I acted. It's not as if he was the one cheating on me, or, in Mike's case, making me the other *woman. He called me "yoga buddy" this morning. It's such a stupid thing, but it's* our *thing—our inside joke. Does Brad realize how one silly phrase connects us? Did he say it deliberately? I need to think.*

Devika went home and meditated, clearing her mind and balancing her emotions. Within her bubble of calm, she weighed her options regarding Brad. She felt her sense of calm wavering, and she adjusted her focus, restoring her peace.

Who am I angry at? Brad or me? Both, but mostly me. I was hurt, and I lashed out. I wasn't fair to Manny and Nelson. I wasn't fair to Brad. I definitely wasn't fair to poor Becca. She deserved to know what kind of monster Mike was, but when I told her, I wasn't thinking of her and her pain. Only my own pain and rage.

I can't make up for everything, but I can make up for some of it.

Devika slowly brought herself out of her meditation, gradually letting the world back in. She sighed and stood up, walking over to her phone.

Devika: *Hi yoga buddy*

Class tomorrow?

She put her phone down and walked toward the kitchen. Devika made it about four steps before her phone buzzed. Turning back, she read the response.

Brad: *Sounds great*

Six ok?

Devika: *Perfect*

Brad: *CU then*

Devika put her phone down and took a deep breath. She once again turned toward the kitchen and lunch.

I can do this. It's just yoga with a friend. I need to apologize to Manny and Nelson, too.

She invited her ex-husband and his fiancé over for dinner to apologize for barging in on them on Friday. They were appreciative and assured her the apology was unnecessary, but they didn't say no to her cooking, either. The three of them spent a nice, relaxing evening together with wine and homemade Indian food. Devika felt better about her relationship with them afterward. Brad was a different story.

Work on Monday presented a new set of challenges. Devika was scheduled to cover a groundbreaking ceremony with the mayor. Last year she'd met Mike for the first time at one of those, and he had been flirty and charming. They'd seen each other a few more times at similar events, and she knew there was a good chance he would be at this one as well.

Devika knocked on her boss' door. "Hey, Craig. Can I come in?"

"Sure, Devika. What's up?"

She closed the door behind her. "Um, any chance you can give someone else the groundbreaking assignment?"

"Can I ask why?"

Devika studied her shoes. "I went on a few dates with one of the mayor's lawyers who often goes to these events. I ended things on Thursday, and I really don't want to risk seeing him there."

"I see. I'm guessing this is related to taking Friday off?"

"Yeah. Sorry."

"While you were here on Friday, you didn't happen to use department resources for personal—" Craig stopped talking and held his hand up, signaling Devika to stay silent. "You know what? Forget I said anything. One of the most important rules of being a manager is to not ask questions you don't want the answer to. It's better for both of us if I don't ask any questions, and as far as anyone is concerned, you were never here on Friday."

"What's—"

"Don't ask. Yes, I'll send Steve. Meanwhile, I want you down at Sea-Tac. I'll text you the assignment on the way."

"Thanks, Craig."

"Don't mention it. And get going. I gotta call Steve and send him halfway across the city in rush hour."

Devika raced over to Sea-Tac to get photos of city workers assisting with the cleanup of a chemical spill. She spent the rest of the day bustling around town.

Craig's a good guy, but I suspect I'm going to get the shit assignments for a while. There's something going on, and I'm pretty sure he's covering for me.

She was late to yoga, walking in during the opening stretches. Devika nodded apologetically to Sam, the instructor, and looked for Brad.

Bless him. Brad staked out some extra space in the corner for me. He saw me. Oh… Wow. The look of relief on his face just now. He must have thought I ditched him.

Brad flashed her a demure smile as he moved his mat over to make room for her. Devika silently mouthed, "Sorry." He nodded in response before turning his attention back to Sam. She noted throughout the class how much his form had improved.

After class, Devika looked at Brad and said, "Sorry I was late."

"That's okay. I'm just glad—never mind."

"You thought I ditched you."

Brad looked contemplative. "I was worried about you."

He had every reason to believe I would ghost him.

"Work was rough today. Thank you for saving me a spot."

Brad chortled. "It wasn't easy. A few people were a bit miffed I was taking up so much space."

Devika looked around at the other students. She saw the looks subtly directed at Brad and at her. Puzzle pieces started falling into place in her mind.

Brad's a single, attractive man who looks like he probably has his shit together—even though I know he doesn't—in a class full of women of a relatively similar age, athleticism, and attractiveness. He's like a steak in a pool full of piranha. Some of the looks I'm getting...wow. I'm pretty sure some of these women are none too happy to see me back in class, especially since they all know he saved me the spot they wanted.

Suddenly feeling an unscratchable itch in her spine, like someone was sizing up her back for the right spot to slip in a dagger, Devika had to force herself not to run. When class was over, she casually walked out next to Brad.

"Are you coming back tomorrow, yoga buddy?"

He grinned. "I can't. I have a coffee date with..." Brad paused to think. "Oh, right. Kristi. Coffee with Kristi."

Forget the dagger in the back, there's a blade in my heart.

"Oh. How's your thing with Kristi going?"

Brad blew a raspberry, and his shoulders slumped. "Online dating is stressful. I've been on a bunch of first dates, but only a couple second dates. Nope. Sorry. Just one second date and she was—yeah, I'm not gonna talk about her with you."

"Was it too good?"

"Nope."

"Oof. Bad?" Devika asked with a sincerity she didn't feel.

"Nope."

"Come on, Brad. You can't leave me hanging," she pleaded.

"Actually, I kinda can. I'm not ready to share just yet."

"Okay, I respect your decision. I shouldn't have pushed."

"It's fine."

Devika gave him the eye, trying to determine if "It's fine" meant nothing or something really bad. Probably nothing.

"So, what's a girl have to do to get a coffee date on your busy social calendar?"

Brad's face was a giddy blend of confusion and excitement. "I'm busy on Tuesday. Wednesday you have the intermediate class—"

"*Wednesday.* Let's do Wednesday. I'll change my class, cancel it, whatever. Wednesday it is."

I don't care if I'm babbling. If he had said Thursday, then I might have had a meltdown on the spot. I don't when I'm going to be able to go out on a Thursday again.

"Oh, great. Wednesday then."

They started walking in different directions down the sidewalk. Devika looked back and saw Brad's fist pump. She grinned and shook her head.

Pretending

Fletcher

The Tuesday coffee date with Kristi was fascinating. She was pretty and lively, with hot-pink hair, about a dozen ear piercings, and a plethora of tattoos. It wasn't a look Brad would have thought he would like, but it worked well for her and he dug her vibe. He had enough fun on the date that he even forgot about Devika for a while. Unfortunately for him, he was a bit too basic for Kristi.

New Brad apparently isn't interesting enough, I guess. Not that Old Brad would have been better. Tomorrow I'll see Devika for our first date. Our first official *date. I wish I knew what to expect.*

Wednesday was a smooth day at work for Brad and his team. His unspoken policy of thinking how his father would handle a personnel situation, then doing the exact opposite, was working well. Brad organized a birthday card, balloons, and cake for Yolanda last week—something he never would have done before. With a happy and relaxed team, the business side of the credit union ran smoothly, and Brad felt good about his management abilities.

He left at his usual time and went home to Cricket, who trotted to meet him. Brad squatted down to pet and scratch her enthusiastically. Cricket matched his energy with her own, rubbing herself against his calves and eagerly headbonking him. His calves cramping, Brad reluctantly stood up. Cricket ran off to the couch, tail held stiffly in the air.

Putting down his coat and bag, Brad grabbed a string toy and started playing with Cricket. Playing kept them both busy until he needed to get ready to meet Devika. He removed his work clothes, replacing them with his ubiquitous jeans, an AC/DC t-shirt, and an open flannel shirt. He brushed his teeth and quickly checked his hair. Satisfied, he set out.

Brad was a couple of minutes early, and Devika was a few minutes late. She arrived looking flustered. "I'm so sorry I'm late."

"It's okay," Brad said soothingly.

She seemed flustered. "How do we do this? The coffee date, I mean."

Brad grinned and stuck his hand out. "Hi, I'm Brad. It's great to finally meet you, Devika."

Rolling her eyes, she gave him a fist to bump, and responded, "Good to meet you as well, Brad. Shall we get drinks?"

"Of course. Please lead the way."

Brad followed Devika to the counter. She stopped and gave him a quizzical look. "How does this work? Do we each buy our own drinks? Or…"

He chuckled. "I'm not an expert, but mostly we get our own. I did get both one time. Honestly, it's up to you."

"Because I'm a woman?"

Brad shrugged. "Essentially, yes. Traditionally, the guy buys both drinks; however, plenty of women prefer to buy their own drinks, for multiple reasons. I want to make sure my dates have agency in this."

Devika cocked an eyebrow. "What are you finding your dates prefer?"

He lifted his shoulders up near his ears before letting them slump. "It's situational. Sometimes she wants me to take charge and buy both drinks, but doesn't say so. I find it frustrating if she doesn't communicate her desire, but whatever. So yeah, I can pay for both of us, we can split, you can buy both. Up to you."

"Interesting. Let's split."

"Perfect."

They gathered their drinks and sat down at a table. "Now what?" Devika asked.

Good question.

"Usually, we would talk about our jobs or hobbies—get to know each other. You and I have covered those subjects already."

"Can we pretend we don't know each other? I feel like we need a fresh start."

"I'd like a do over. Do you want me to start?"

Devika looked at him shyly. "Yes. I'd like it if you kicked us off." Pursing her lips, she queried, "Tell me about yourself, Brad."

Brad smiled gently. "I'm new to Seattle, just moved here about a month ago after my divorce. I recently started doing yoga for the first time."

Devika smirked. "How's yoga going?"

"Oof. Not gonna lie. It was a rough start because I was stupid and overconfident and decided to skip the beginner classes and went straight to intermediate." Brad stopped and grinned coyly. "I got really lucky, though. I met a yoga buddy who took pity on me. She's really made a difference—she's helped me get my shit together."

Devika nodded. "She sounds incredible."

Brad agreed. "Incredible is the perfect word."

"So, I have to ask, Brad. If this yoga buddy is so perfect, why are you going out on coffee dates rather than dating your yoga buddy?" Devika's eyes narrowed.

Because I'm a moron, a coward, and an asshole. Now is the time to fix everything, if I can. I can feel the heat in my temples and the flush in my cheeks. My entire body is sweaty, yet there's a ball of ice in the pit of my stomach.

"You ask an extremely difficult question." Brad took a deep breath. *Here goes everything.* His words tumbled out with his ragged exhalation. "I've made a lot of mistakes in my life. Many of them recently. I feel like a damaged person, and I worry I'm going to hurt my yoga buddy. Also, on New Year's Eve, I told her everything about my past and just how awful I was. I'm worried that I scared her, in part because recounting all of my mistakes scared me." Brad took a sip. His mouth felt so dry. "The crazy thing is—it seemed to me she shied away at first, but then we spent this magical time just standing and watching the ferries together. It was perfect and beautiful, just like my yoga buddy."

"Perfect *and* beautiful." Devika's voice was as hard as iron, but brittle. Brad could practically hear the cracks spider-webbing behind the façade. "What happened then?"

Brad exhaled. Keeping his voice meticulously modest, he continued, "Midnight came, and we were encouraged to share a New Year's kiss. My yoga buddy's lips were magical. Electric. Soft and warm. Terrifying."

"Terrifying?" The iron voice was even harder, yet more brittle.

"Yes. I was terrified of how I felt. Of how I thought she might feel about me. Most of all, my anxieties and self-doubt flooded my head, and the fear of the Old Brad frightened me to my core. So, like the coward I am, I pulled back."

"I see." The iron shattered, and Devika hid her face behind her cup. They stayed like this for what seemed like an eternity, using coffee cups as masks. Finally, Devika broke their reflective silence. "What happened then?"

"I think I hurt her badly at the moment. Soon after, my yoga buddy told me she was going on a date with someone else. I tried to be cheerful for her, but I just felt pain inside. She deserved better than me, or at least that's what I told myself. Things were just so different, and I didn't handle it well. Then I started going on dates as well."

"Can I ask you something?"

"Of course. Anything."

"You told me about a promise you made. The next woman you slept with would be someone you would want to introduce to Sophia. Did you keep your promise?"

"Yes. I have. I also promised to become the man my daughter thinks I am. And I intend to keep *all* of my promises."

Devika nodded her head. So softly it was almost imperceptible, she asked, "What about your yoga buddy?"

Is she asking what I think the status of our relationship is? Is she asking if I want to sleep with her? Is she asking something else entirely?

"I'm not sure. It seems like she's been through a lot of pain recently. I think my past reminds her of her pain. I want to support her and be there for her. At the same time, I don't want to hurt her, and if she needs space, then I'll give her space. I just don't know what to do."

Devika's chair squealed on the floor as she thrust her hips backward. She sprang up and grabbed her coat. "I'm sorry, Brad. Don't hate me." Devika ran for the exit, tears streaming down her face. Brad was barely halfway standing by the time she flung open the door, disappearing into the dismal Seattle night.

He looked around, chagrined as he noted everyone staring at him. Brad gave an apologetic and embarrassed shrug, cleared the table, and left. *Well, I don't think that went well.*

Chapter 28
Amour
The Warning

*S*hit, shit, shit, shit, shit. He must think I'm insane or I hate him. Or both. Probably both. Manny and Nelson were right—I should have talked to him weeks ago. I was hurt and proud and defensive. Like tonight.

I'm still raw from that asshole, Mike's, treachery. Then, to top it off, Brad just explained what he was thinking on New Year's, his fears, and how he felt like a coward. How did I respond to him baring his soul? I asked him if he had sex with any of those women. Like his sex life fucking matters, or I'm in a place to criticize him. A week *ago, I was debating risking another round of pregnancy roulette with a serial adulterer. And then my final question—"What about your yoga buddy?" What was I thinking?*

I have to do something. I have to try and fix this.

Devika stopped under a shop awning to keep her phone dry and opened her messaging app. She texted Brad.

Devika: *I'm sorry. Can I make it up to you?*

Dinner Saturday?

Brad: *I can't do Saturday*

I'll be in Portland to see Sophia

Friday night?

Devika: *Friday it is*

Brad: *Are you ok?*

Devika: *I'll be good. Just a lot to process right now*

I'm sorry

Brad: *Don't be sorry*

> *I understand*

> *Please text me when you get home so I know you're safe*

> Devika: *I will*

> *Thank you*

> Brad: *You're welcome*

Devika put her phone away and hurried back into the wet Seattle night. Once home, she texted Brad as promised, ate some leftovers, and watched some women's hockey. She wasn't entirely sure of all the rules, but it was fun to watch. Devika meditated before going to bed, hoping her routine would help keep her thoughts sorted. It didn't work.

Brad shared the truth about his infidelity with me on New Year's. How painful was it for him to admit that, and how vulnerable did he feel? Yeah, I opened up and made myself vulnerable, too. But it's different. He completely ruined his life with his decisions.

So there he is, in a quiet corner of a party, talking with a woman he calls incredible—me—and I ask why he's really in Seattle. He could have told me it was none of my business. I even gave him a way out. Instead, Brad voluntarily risks everything for the brutal truth. We get through his disclosure, I say my thing, then we have our long glorious moment. I never considered just how much his confession affected him. His explanation of the botched kiss makes so much sense. I just didn't think of any of that at the moment. Oh, right. Because I was still feeling vulnerable after what I said.

Instead of talking with Brad, I went out with Mike. Two terrible decisions in a row. Then tonight, I ran out on him in tears. I'm going to fix it, though. Friday night, I will start making amends. Next task—figure out what making amends even means.

Just thinking of tears had Devika crying again. She cried herself to sleep later.

Waking up on Thursday morning, she briefly considered calling out, but decided being alone all day wouldn't make things better. Devika stopped by the office to check in with Craig about an assignment.

"Hey, Craig. About the youth sports facilities—"

"Close the door and take a seat."

Uh-oh. That's never good.

"Have you heard?"

Devika looked at Craig quizzically. "Heard what?"

"Scandal in the mayor's office."

Uh-oh again.

Craig continued, "Apparently one of the mayor's lawyers was boning a city councilman's wife. You wouldn't—never mind. I don't want to know."

"Um. I hadn't heard anything."

"Well, you'll probably hear the full scoop soon. He had a fiancée who just dumped him. Oh, he was also involved with the chief of staff's daughter, at least two law students at UW, and the wife of the mayor's biggest donor."

I feel sick now.

"Please tell me the chief of staff's daughter is an adult."

"She is now. Apparently, the police are investigating when their relationship started." Craig looked at her and asked kindly, "Are you okay? You look like you might need the day off."

Devika waved him off. "Without getting into details, let me assure you I would *much* rather be working today."

"I get it. Normally I would offer to talk with you, but it's better I can tell any potential investigators the truth. I know nothing about any possible misuse of department resources for personal use, and I'm insulted at the implication."

"Got it. Has anyone—"

"Let's just focus on your assignment today."

"Sorry. Thanks, Craig."

"No problem, Devika. I'll admit I'm being a bit selfish about this. Replacing you with someone of equal ability would be a giant pain in my ass." He grinned at her.

Devika saw Brad at yoga later in the evening. They went through the class side-by-side. She even took advantage of a couple opportunities to check out his ass. After class, Devika clinked water bottles with Brad, saying, "Thank you for sharing during our coffee date last night. I appreciate you opening up like you did."

"You're welcome."

"I have a lot going on emotionally and felt overwhelmed yesterday. It wasn't your fault."

"Devika, I understand."

"I appreciate your courage. Tomorrow, would you like to eat down around the waterfront and watch the ferries?"

Brad's grin was ear-to-ear. "Is watching the ferries a thing for us?"

"Maybe it is. You don't mind?"

"Not at all. If you don't mind me saying, I think it's a perfect date."

"All right. Can I text you where and when tomorrow?"

"Sure."

"Okay. I'm gonna head out."

"Have a good night, Devika. I'll need to snuggle Cricket extra hard tonight to make up for tomorrow."

Chapter 29

Alone

Heart

"All right, little lady. I need your help picking out something to wear."

Cricket completely ignored him, choosing instead to walk around his closet.

"You're not helpful." Brad sighed.

Tonight feels important, and I want to dress for it. I should look nice, but not too fancy. Not too casual. I could wear a work shirt, but I don't feel like it's me.

Brad pulled out a flannel and a polo and laid them on the bed. He took a quick shower and shaved off the five o'clock shadow. Back in the bedroom, Cricket was curled up and sleeping on his flannel. "Polo shirt it is. Thank you for helping me choose." Brad pulled on the polo and jeans before checking the mirror.

I'm so glad I didn't cut myself shaving.

He laced up his Doc Martens and walked to the kitchen to feed Cricket. Brad didn't know how long the date would go, so he didn't want to worry about feeding her. She mewled appreciatively before shoving her face into the bowl. Cricket inhaled her food, and Brad waited a few minutes to make sure she didn't bring it all back up again. Satisfied she was digesting well, he cooed goodnight to her, and walked out. He caught a bus headed downtown, and meditated to keep himself centered.

Brad was a couple minutes early, but Devika was already standing there. She noticed him coming, and they waved to each other. "Hi. Sorry, I hope you weren't waiting long."

Devika looped her arm into his. "Nope. Not long at all. Is this okay?" She nodded at their arms with a hopeful expression.

"Definitely."

They stayed arm-in-arm until they were seated. Devika sat down first, and Brad sat opposite her. After the hostess left, Devika patted the seat next to her, saying, "Brad, would you like to sit next to me?"

"Sure." He quickly changed seats.

"Perfect. Now we can both watch the ferries come and go." A massive ferry was pulling in, probably laden with Friday night evening-goers from Bainbridge Island.

This is definitely a thing for us.

They decided what to order and turned back to watching the ferry's crew direct the offloading process. "I'm really sorry again about running out on you Wednesday," Devika said quietly.

"Don't be sorry. Emotions can be a challenge for all of us. How do you feel now?"

"Anxious. Happy. Scared."

"Me too. Do you want to talk about it?"

Devika expelled a deep breath. "Not yet. After she takes our order." She moved her hand until her fingers grazed the small hairs on the back of his hand. Brad twisted and opened up his hand in invitation, and she slid her hand into his. They sat silently like that until the waitress came back for the orders.

After she left, Devika sighed. "I screwed up. I mean...I screwed up a lot. This entire month, I've just made one terrible mistake after another."

"Just to be clear, does this count?"

Brad's attempt at levity fell flat.

Devika's voice sounded eggshell thin as she answered, "Maybe. The night is still young."

"Sorry. I shouldn't have said anything."

"It's okay, Brad. I appreciate the thought." Devika paused. Brad recognized the rhythm of breathing exercises and joined her. "All right, better. Going back to New Year's, I was a mess that night. Your confession upset me, and then I told you about my stupid mistakes, I guess to make you feel like you weren't alone in screwing up. I don't know. Anyway, I was feeling vulnerable and upset, but also so happy for Manny and Nelson. Plus, I was feeling connected with you, even though I was still kinda angry and repulsed as well."

Ouch. Understandable, but still painful.

"And then you pulled back from our kiss, and everything just fell apart. In retrospect, we should have talked, but instead I ran. There was this hot guy who flirted with me a bunch and asked me out around the holidays. So, I contacted him, and we went out to this really nice place, and it was sexy and romantic. At the end of the night, he kissed me, and it was so much better than our kiss. I wanted so badly to see him again, but he told me he had plans, so I had to wait a week for another date. He took me to this jazz club, which was also sexy and romantic. I think I had one glass of wine, but at the end of the night, I was drunk and horny..."

Oh no. I don't want to hear this.

Devika took a big gulp of water before continuing. "I was on my period, or else I would have slept with him. It was the weekend of the storm, so we didn't see each other again. Then I had to wait until Thursday to see him again. He let me choose the date, so I invited him over for dinner and sex. Well, dinner, but I planned to fuck him all night. Right before dinner, I saw text messages from another woman on his phone."

Brad had been getting angrier and angrier throughout Devika's tale. Not at her, but at himself, and even more so, at this Mike asshole. Brad let out an angry rumble, and Devika flinched. He shoved his anger down, saying, "I'm really sorry, Devika. That guy is a cheating shitweasel."

"You sound really angry."

"I mean…yeah, I'm pissed off." He saw her expression and quickly added, "Not at you. I'm pissed off at him—and at me."

"I don't understand."

"This fucker was manipulating you from the start. I know for sure, because he did just what I would have done at one time."

"What?"

Brad took a deep breath and blew it out. "Look, some girls are easy, and you don't really have to work to get in their pants. Someone like you, though—you're smart, sophisticated, worldly. For a player, it's hard to go after your weaknesses, so you target your strengths instead. Let me guess, the first restaurant was upscale but not excessively fancy."

"Yeah, that's a good description."

"You have to be fancy enough to impress, but not so posh as to look like you're trying too hard. I assume he already had other women, so he stuck you on Thursday in his rotation. Then, the jazz club. Again, upscale and classy. You probably did have one glass of wine, but I bet he slipped the waiter some cash to make sure your glass was always topped up while you were distracted."

"Motherfucker."

"If the alcohol doesn't get you in the sack, then he sets the hook. He gives you the choice of date three, knowing you aren't likely to outdo the first two dates. The idea is to unsettle you to make you vulnerable, paving the way for the seduction. Quick question, was he late for every date?"

Devika looked at him quizzically. "Yes, why?"

"That's a play. Don't be late enough to piss her off, but just late enough to throw her off balance and ensure she's anticipating you."

"*Holy shit.* That's awful."

Brad hung his head in shame. "I know. It's all terrible and manipulative. I'm so sorry."

"You didn't do it."

"Not to you, no. There's a reason I know all this shit, though. I'm reliving all the horrible things I've done." Brad could feel tears welling in his eyes.

Devika squeezed his hand. "Hey. Look at me."

He did.

"Are you being manipulative now?" Devika asked.

"No..."

"Are you ever going to do it again?"

Brad shook his head vehemently.

"You can't change your past. You can learn from it and be better, though."

"That's what I'm doing, I swear."

"I believe you. I know admitting your past was hard for you. It was hard for me to listen to it—to know how I got played."

"I'm so sorry. I was so wrapped up in my feelings, I forgot to ask about you."

"It's okay—"

"No, it's not. You were taken advantage of, and I should have been more cognizant of your feelings." Brad rumbled again. "I want to kick his ass."

Devika laughed. "Men."

"What?"

"You don't have to. He's already taken care of. I outed him to his fiancée, and he's now lost his job because he was screwing a city councilman's wife."

Realization struck. "Yolanda was telling me about this yesterday. That was Mike?"

"Yeah."

"What a scumbag."

"Yeah…"

Further discussion was temporarily halted by the arrival of their appetizers—two steaming cups of clam chowder. Grateful for the distraction, they both dug in.

Bowl clean, Brad pushed it back. "That tastes so good."

"It really is." Devika was scraping out the last bits from her bowl.

"Can we take a break from the past for a while? I feel exhausted."

"Me, too. What would you like to talk about?"

"I'd like to talk about the future, if that's okay with you," Brad said shyly.

"All right. I'd prefer something positive." Devika was smiling.

"Let me start by saying I'm a mess—"

"Oh, I'm well aware," Devika teased him.

Brad leaned back in mock offense. "Hey, no need to agree so quickly. You could have at least tried to deny it."

Devika laughed, and he laughed, too.

It's nice to see her smile again.

"I don't want to go too fast."

"Understandable."

"More than anything, I really don't want to mess this up." Brad paused. "Just to be clear, I want to explore a deeper relationship with you, and I'm terrified of screwing up."

"Yeah, I definitely empathize. You're the best yoga buddy I've ever had."

"Oh my god..."

They both giggled. Before Brad could continue, the waitress arrived with dinner.

Brad looked over his plate at the retreating ferry. "Want to continue this after we eat?"

"Good plan."

Once finished, they watched as the Bainbridge Island ferry docked, passengers and crew scurrying about. Brad felt Devika's hand infiltrating his again. The waitress cleared their plates, asking about dessert or coffee. Brad looked at Devika, who shrugged. Looking back at the waitress, he declined and asked for the check.

Not long after, they walked arm-in-arm back into the damp Seattle night. They strolled along the sidewalk, silently enjoying each other's company. As they approached the Pike Place Market, Devika dragged Brad to a halt under a covered area. He looked at her—wet, bedraggled, and somehow still beautiful anyway.

"I want to try something," Devika said, her voice husky. She lifted onto her tiptoes, leaning toward him, lips pursed. Brad tilted his head down to meet her, and they kissed for the second time. Unlike the first time, Brad didn't pull back, but instead let her lips linger upon his for as long as she wanted. Those lips felt heavenly—soft, warm, and sensual.

They heard a cough, and someone nearby said, "Get a room." The spell broke, and they pulled apart, eyes locked together.

Devika spoke softly, "Brad, I need to say three things. First, I want to explore a deeper relationship with you. Second, sex is off the table for the foreseeable future." She stopped.

"I like the first thing, and I'm not really ready for the second thing anyway, so I accept. What's the third thing?"

"It's hard to say because I feel very vulnerable, but I also need to say it *because* I feel so vulnerable." Devika took a deep breath. "I don't want to be alone tonight."

Chapter 30

Hold Me Now

Thompson Twins

She could see the explosion of emotions on Brad's face as her words sunk in. His expression settled into one of longing. His voice sounded raw when he said, "Me neither." Brad seemed to gather his thoughts before continuing, "Whatever makes you most comfortable is good with me, okay? I'll let you lead."

"You should be comfortable, too."

"True. Thank you."

"Did you drive?"

"No, I took the bus."

"I drove. Want to take my car?"

"Sure."

They walked the short distance to Devika's car, and she drove to Brad's place. As she parked, she noticed the quizzical expression on his face. She turned the car off and faced him.

Brad said softly, "Thank you for trusting me."

"You're welcome. Honestly, my place has felt weird for the past week."

He smiled kindly. "I hope this is more comfortable, then."

They walked up to his door, which Brad gingerly opened. He looked around, then quickly entered, almost dragging her behind him. As he shut the door, he apologized. "Sorry. I'm deathly afraid Cricket will run out."

"Makes sense. Where is she?"

"I'm not sure. I think she's nervous. I haven't had anyone else in here since..."

"Since I helped you bring her home?"

"Yeah. Hopefully she remembers you."

"Um, the place looks nice."

Brad chuckled. "Thank you for saying so. It still feels pretty bare." He sighed. "Megan was always better at decorating, and making a house into a home. My last piece of art was a poster of a woman in a g-string next to a sports car on my wall in college."

Devika smirked. "Classy."

He snorted in response. "Yeah. Megan made me get rid of it."

"Don't take this the wrong way, but I rather like your ex-wife." Devika kept her voice light and grinned to show she was teasing.

"Come on, let's sit on the couch." He led her over and sat down. "Honestly, I think you and Megan would like each other."

"Really?"

"Yeah."

Devika teased him, "Are you saying you have a type?"

She watched silently as he pulled out a toy and dangled it in front of the couch. He looked, and after a minute, a tiny paw snaked out to bat at the toy. Brad lowered the toy back down and sighed. "I think I do have a type. Incredibly intelligent, devastatingly beautiful women who do yoga."

"I mean...that's not a bad type to have."

"It's not—oh, there she is." Brad put the toy away as Cricket emerged. The little cat hopped up onto his lap, purring and head-bonking him. After a short amount of time, Cricket wandered over to Devika's lap, nuzzling her before settling down her legs. "I see how it is, you little traitor." Brad smiled affectionately at Cricket as he said this.

"Aw, leave her alone. She's showing her guest hospitality."

"Speaking of hospitality, I didn't offer you a drink or anything."

Brad panicked until Devika said, "It's okay, although I wouldn't mind a glass of water."

He sprung up and filled a glass for her. Bringing it back, he handed it to her before sitting down again. "We do this every night, for a couple of minutes or a couple of hours. I sit down, and Cricket gets in my lap."

"Every night?"

"Yes. It's our thing. I'm really sad about missing it tomorrow."

"Right, Portland. Is someone watching her?"

"Nelson said—" He stopped when Devika snorted.

"Let me take care of her. Nelson is completely useless with animals. I'll text him."

"Uh, sure. I guess."

"I promise I'll take good care of Cricket."

Brad looked relieved. "Thank you. I'll admit, I was a bit nervous about Nelson, but I figured one night and one morning couldn't hurt."

Devika perked up. "You're staying overnight?"

"It's too late to get the train back. I figure I'll find a hotel. If I'm lucky, I might even get a last-minute discount."

"So, you liked the train suggestion?"

"I did. It will be fun to try it out."

Devika softly stroked Cricket's fur. *I like this. It feels comfortable and beats another lonely night at home.*

"Is this your reading pile?" Devika nodded at a haphazard stack of non-fiction.

"Yep. All mine."

"You aren't going in for light reading, are you?"

Brad pursed his lips. "No. Some of these are Tasha's suggestions, and others I found. One of my goals is to educate myself."

"I can see. I recognize *Caste*. Hey, do you have a book on sex?"

"Sex and relationships. Like I said, trying to educate myself."

"Question for you—how much of this honest and vulnerable thing is actually you?"

"For the Old Brad, none of it. New Brad is learning and trying new things. Still a work in progress, but better every day."

Devika considered his answer. "Okay, next question—how long do you stay on the couch with Cricket?"

"Until it's bedtime. I did fall asleep with her a few times, though. Are you getting tired?"

"I am."

"All right. You can have the bed, and I'll take the couch."

"Brad?"

"Yeah?"

"No one is sleeping on the couch. Do you have a shirt I can borrow?"

"Let me grab a couple. You can pick."

A few minutes later, she was standing in his bedroom, looking at t-shirts while he nervously held a new toothbrush in his hand. "I've got more shirts, if needed, and one of those toothbrushes the dentist always gives you."

Devika selected a shirt and took the offered toothbrush, walking into the bathroom. When she emerged, wearing his Green Day shirt, Brad was standing on the far side of the room in a t-shirt and athletic shorts. "I don't bite," she said.

"I know. I just want to give you space."

"Thank you, you're kind. The bathroom is all yours."

"Okay." Brad tried to glide past her, but Devika moved to intercept him.

Her hand resting lightly on his chest, she asked, "Can I get a kiss?"

Brad leaned down and kissed her tenderly. Devika melted into his mouth.

"Thank you," she said, pulling back. Devika slid under the covers as Brad closed the bathroom door.

When he emerged, he stood in the bathroom doorway and asked, "Are you sure you're comfortable with sleeping here?"

This is crazy, but I need it.

"I am. Are you?"

"I think so."

"Tell me if you aren't, okay?"

"I will."

"You promise?"

"I promise."

"Good, because I heard New Brad always keeps his promises."

He walked around the bed and slid under the covers.

"Brad? Hold me now."

"Yeah, what can I—"

Devika slithered over, tucking herself under his arm and resting her head on his chest. "Thank you." Within minutes, she was fast asleep.

Chapter 31
Don't Stop Believin'
Journey

Brad woke up on Saturday morning with an aching back and neck. At some point in the night, Devika had rolled off of him and was sleeping on the far side of the bed. Brad gave himself a few minutes for his raging case of morning wood to subside before he got out of bed.

Old Brad would have found another use for his morning wood. New Brad is going to go and get coffee...except I don't remember what Devika drinks. Okay, new plan. New Brad is going to wow Devika with a homemade breakfast of—Brad opened the fridge and found disappointment—*yogurt and granola. That isn't going to impress her.*

As Brad fixed Cricket her breakfast and deliberated what to do for Devika and himself, he heard a noise. He looked up to see Devika walk in while stretching languidly. The Green Day shirt rode up, exposing pink panties.

Holy shit...

Devika padded toward him, eyes sparkling under a tangled thicket of bedhead. She lifted up on her toes to plant a gentle kiss on his lips. "Thank you for last night."

You know what? I'm good with morning breath. Oh gosh, I hope mine isn't too bad.

"You're welcome. How did you sleep?"

"Incredible. I haven't slept that well in a very long time." Devika smiled contentedly.

"I'm glad to hear it. I didn't snore too loudly, did I?"

"If you did, then I didn't notice. I got used to Manny anyway—he sounds like New Delhi Train Station when he sleeps. You're fine."

"Whew. Good to know."

"Did Megan complain about your snoring?"

"Sometimes. Not as often as I should have complained about *her* snoring."

"Megan snores? Wow. Somehow that makes me want to meet her even more."

"Oh no! Please don't tell her I told you she snores."

"*Brad Kowalski.* You look genuinely panicked right now." Devika tapped a fingernail on her wickedly grinning lips. "Now I have to figure out what you'll need to do to buy my silence."

"You're just cruel." Brad mock pouted. "I'll go and get us coffee and breakfast."

"Do you have time? When is your train?"

"I have about three hours."

"What do you have here?"

"Um, yogurt and granola."

"Tell you what, let's have yogurt and hit the early morning yoga class. I'll just have to run home and change."

"Sounds like a good plan."

Devika gave him a shy look. "Brad, are you okay with last night? You know. Me sleeping in your bed, but no sex?"

Brad responded immediately and emphatically, "*Yes.* I really liked it. You can sleep here any time you want." He paused before adding. "It's been over two months since I last had sex. That's when Megan caught me. Right now, I feel like it is better for me if we keep our relationship platonic."

"Platonic works for me as well. My toys might get worn out, though."

Brad waggled his eyebrows. "What kind of toys?"

Devika slapped him on the arm. "Behave. Now give me a kiss, and let's eat breakfast."

"Your wish is my command, my lady."

They spent an enjoyable morning together until Brad needed to get ready to depart for Portland. He gave Devika his spare key and a note with instructions for Cricket's care.

A few hours later, he arrived at Portland's Union Station. Brad walked over to where Megan's texts instructed him and saw her Subaru. Megan and Tasha occupied the two front seats, so Brad piled into the back with Sophia.

"Hi, Daddy!"

"Hi, sweetheart. Hi, Megan and Tasha. Thank you for picking me up."

"You're welcome," Megan said.

"Good to see you, Brad."

Wow, Tasha even sounded like she meant it. I'm shocked, but perhaps I shouldn't be. I'm happy to see all three of them.

"Good to see you, too, Tasha."

"Daddy, who is watching Cricket while you are gone?"

"Daddy's new friend, Devika, is watching her." Brad saw Megan's glance in the rearview mirror and noted her eyebrows lifting at his response.

"Is Devika nice?" Sophia asked.

Brad answered, "Yes, she is very nice, and she promised to take good care of Cricket." He could see Megan's eyebrows testing the limits of physics.

Last Megan heard, I had royally screwed up with Devika. She didn't want to talk then but seems curious now.

"Yes, Brad. Tell us about your yoga buddy," Tasha drawled.

"Maybe not right now. How's the new business going, Tasha?"

She grunted at his deflection but answered him. "Great. I have a ton of new clients."

"That's wonderful. I'm really happy for you."

And somewhat surprisingly, I mean it.

The four of them ate an early dinner before roller derby, chatting about safe topics, most of which revolved around Sophia. Sophia enjoyed her first two adult roller derby bouts immensely, and Brad treasured the opportunity to share in her excitement. She was tired by the end, as this was past her normal bed time.

Megan dropped Sophia and Tasha off at their place and drove Brad over to his hotel. "So, what's going on with your yoga buddy?"

"Thank you for asking, Megan." He twisted in his seat to look at her. "I don't want to start a fight, but feel like I should ask this first. Last time we spoke, you didn't want to know about my love life. Is this a question you want me to answer?"

He could see her stiffen at first and then relax. "Am I overstepping?" Megan asked with a sigh. "I do want to know how you're doing, and part of that seems to involve her—Devika."

"No, it's okay. I'm honestly doing all right. I feel like every day I'm wallowing in my past a little less, and learning from it a little more. Devika...truthfully, I'm not entirely sure what is going on with us. She just had her heart broken by the biggest asshole in Seattle. I'm still processing my extensive list of fuck-ups, and our divorce. We're both lonely and vulnerable."

"In other words, it's complicated."

"It is. But we're trying to support each other and nurture our own relationship."

"Good to hear. Tell me more about her."

"Obviously, we met through yoga. She's a photographer for the Seattle government. She likes hiking and skiing, not interested in camping. Her favorite part of hiking is the opportunity to take pictures. She's smart and funny. Oh, our favorite activity is sitting and watching the ferries going in and out of Seattle."

"Seriously? You just sit and watch big boats docking?"

"Yeah. It's kinda Zen. Oh, she taught me how to meditate."

"And do you meditate?"

"Every day."

Megan belly laughed. "I *have* to meet the woman who got Brad Kowalski doing yoga and meditation *and* who sits and watches the ferries with you."

"Funny you should say that. She keeps saying she wants to meet you, too."

Megan thought for a moment. "How do you feel about the two of us meeting?"

"I think I'm okay. I'm not sure about Devika meeting Tasha, though. My entire world might explode."

Megan laughed in a genuine way, reminding him of how she used to laugh back in college. He felt a surge of remorse for his mistreatment of her, sprinkled with gratitude for her new life and love.

"Speaking of Tasha, how are you two doing?"

"We're excellent. Actually, we're thinking of getting married on Memorial Day weekend." She glanced at him. "Would you come if we invited you?"

He sniffled, and the world outside the car dimmed as his eyes watered. "I would be honored. I'm so happy for you. Both of you."

"Brad, are you crying?"

"Yes."

"You jackass! You didn't even cry at our wedding." Megan struggled to stop laughing. Once she calmed down a bit, she said, "Brad, I can't tell you how happy I am that you're getting your shit together. Now get out and go call your yoga buddy."

At least she's smiling. I guess she does approve of Devika.

"Goodnight, Megan. It was great seeing you again."

"Goodnight, Brad. Don't fuck it up again."

"Will do."

Brad got out of Megan's car and walked into his hotel. Once up in his room, he video-called Devika.

"Hi, Brad. Look who I have." She panned the camera down to her lap, where Cricket was curled into a little ball with a paw draped over her face.

"Hey, Devika. I see you two are having a good time."

"We are. Cricket told me she needed her evening lap time, so I'm helping her out."

"That's great, thank you."

"How'd everything go?"

He nodded his head, recalling the day. "Wonderful. We had a lot of fun. I'm so glad I had the chance to see Sophia again. Oh, and Megan wants to meet you."

Devika tittered. "I can't wait. We should have a girls night."

"Um..."

"Aw, you're worried we'd spend all night talking about you behind your back." She paused for effect. "It's more fun to talk about you while you're there."

Brad shook his head in defeat.

"Why don't you tell me more tomorrow?"

"Sounds good. Goodnight, Devika. Goodnight, Cricket."

"Night, Brad."

Chapter 32

Blind Faith

Warrant

B rad got home late Sunday morning to find a happy Cricket purring to greet him. They bonded for a few minutes before he went into his bedroom to hang up his coat. As he was about to turn out the light and close the door, Brad noticed there were dresses in his closet. A quick look in the bathroom revealed the appearance of a new soap, shampoo, and conditioner. He walked back into his bedroom and went to his dresser. One drawer now had decidedly feminine underwear and his Green Day shirt inside. Brad was reaching for his phone when he heard his front door open.

Entering the main room, he saw Devika standing near the door, with two coffees in her hands. She was wearing skinny jeans and his Def Leppard shirt under her winter coat.

"Hi," Brad said. "Can I ask what's going on?"

"Remember yesterday when you told me I could sleep here any time I want?"

Did I say that? I think I did.

"Yeah."

"I might have taken you up on your offer."

"As in, you slept here last night."

Devika put the coffees down and rushed over to embrace him. "I'm sorry, Brad. I was feeling really lonely, and sleeping in your bed—on your pillow—I just didn't feel so alone."

"I'm glad you felt better." He punctuated his remark with a kiss.

"I won't sleep here Tuesday night, I promise, but can I sleep here again tonight?"

"Of course. I missed you last night." He eyed her up and down. "Devika, why are you wearing my shirt?"

She kissed him, then flounced toward the coffees. She handed him one—it was his usual order. "Brad, it's so cute how you think any of your shirts are still yours."

And so their new life began. Devika started sleeping over every Thursday, or sometimes he'd stay at her place. Brad missed her terribly on the nights they were apart, but they'd agreed that it was healthy to maintain some space, even if they both hated it, so they made sure to sleep alone on Tuesdays and Wednesdays.

They went on coffee dates, regular dates, and hikes. They went to museums and the public library. A couple times, they took the ferry over to Bainbridge Island and beyond, into the Olympic Mountains or out to Port Angeles. One day they both took off work for some mid-week skiing.

For five weeks they did this, having fun but never defining their relationship. Then came the first Sunday in March. Brad went down to Portland again for junior roller derby, and he had a good time with Sophia, Megan, and Tasha. Then, as Megan was dropping Brad off at Union Station, she once again said those fateful words. "Brad, don't fuck it up."

When he got back to Seattle, Devika was waiting for him outside the station. He waved to her and walked to her car. She greeted him with a cheerful kiss.

"Hi, how was it?" Devika asked.

"It was good. We had a great time. Sophia told me how her practices were going. She has this friend she goes to practice and school with. I'm so happy for her."

"So—why does something feel off?"

"Megan said something to me as she was dropping me off. She told me not to fuck this up. By which she meant us."

Devika looked concerned. "What did she mean?"

Brad shrugged. "I've been trying to figure it out for almost four hours now."

"We can talk more at home. I made dinner."

Brad's stomach rumbled at the thought. "Awesome."

The smell of *saag aloo* and *vindaloo* chicken when they walked through the door elicited another growl from his belly. "It smells amazing."

She tossed him a self-satisfied smirk. "Of course it does. I made *vindaloo,* and before you ask, I dialed down the spice level for you."

He resisted the sudden urge to kiss her, instead opting to respond by saying, "You're the best."

On a full stomach, Brad prepared to risk it all. "Devika, I've enjoyed all the time we've spent together lately, and I want to make this official. You'll always be my yoga buddy, but I'd like you to be my girlfriend as well."

She looked sick when I started, then terrified, and now I have no idea what she's thinking. I hope I didn't fuck this up. Like Megan warned me not to do.

Devika took a deep breath and said, "Thank you for asking. I've been thinking the same thing, but everything has been so good between us, and I didn't want to mess it all up."

Brad couldn't help but give a sigh of relief. "It was so comfortable. I mean, it still can be."

"There are some things we need to discuss if we're going to make this official."

Don't panic. You've got this, Brad.

"What do you have in mind?" Brad asked.

"When we started rebuilding our relationship, you told me you weren't ready for sex yet. How do you feel now?"

Good question. Don't panic. Just be honest.

Brad looked her in the eyes. "I don't know. I still feel a tremendous amount of guilt and shame around sex." He paused and closed his eyes, focusing on his breathing. "My best answer right now is I would like to push my boundaries a bit. I—"

"Pushing boundaries sounds...oh, I'm sorry. I thought you were done."

"Almost. Sorry. I wanted to say that if we both want to open our relationship to include sex, then I want to talk more about what our comfort levels are before we do anything."

Devika seemed giddy. "Yes, I would like to have sex with you, and I want to respect your boundaries. Whenever you want, we can talk before actually, you know, doing it." She gave him a big, passionate kiss. "On to the next topic?"

"Sure."

"I like our current sleeping arrangements because I'm not entirely sure about moving in together. I haven't lived with anyone except Manny. I hate sleeping alone two nights a week, but I'm worried about whether I can successfully live with someone."

"Ugh, I hate those nights alone, too. What if we did a trial move-in? We pick one of our places and both live together for a month?"

She smiled. "Do you have a preference?"

"I guess I prefer it here, just so I don't have to uproot Cricket."

Devika giggled. "I was thinking the same thing."

Brad couldn't help himself—he stood up, pulling Devika along with him, and he lifted her into a kiss. She wrapped her legs around his hips and kissed him back. Their tongues glided and danced across each other's teeth and tongue. Eventually, Brad's arms tired, and he let her down reluctantly.

"Devika, I love you." Suddenly, Brad's weary arms were again filled with a woman intent on kissing the life out of him.

Devika pulled back long enough to say, "Brad, I love you, too." Then she stuck her tongue so far into Brad's mouth he thought she might reach his larynx.

Exhausted, they separated again. Panting, Devika said, "One last thing to discuss before I say yes to being your girlfriend."

"Sure, anything."

"I want to meet Megan."

Chapter 33
Learning To Fly
Pink Floyd

Devika's words seemed to hang in the air. Brad looked stunned, still panting from their last kiss.

Why did I say I wanted to meet Megan? It just popped in my head, and before I knew it, it came out of my mouth. Did I just ruin everything? I'll tell him it was a joke.

"Yes. Of course." He reached out to gently caress her cheek. "Just to clarify, will you say yes to being my girlfriend now, or do you need to meet Megan first?"

"Now. Definitely now. Honestly, I don't have to meet Megan. I don't even know why I said it."

"Devika, it's okay. You two will have to meet eventually."

"Why?"

"Because you should meet Megan first, before I introduce you to Sophia."

Devika grasped at Brad's arms to steady herself. He responded by gripping her firmly, holding her while her knees remembered how to work again.

"That might be the hottest thing anyone has ever said to me."

"Really? Because I—"

"Yes, you big oaf." Devika gave him a playful smack on the arm. "If you're willing to get Megan's permission for me to meet Sophia, then I must mean a lot to you."

"You mean everything," Brad said tenderly.

"Thank you. I love you. Want to come to bed with me?"

"Uh…"

"To sleep. It's getting late. I'm tired, and you had a long day of traveling and roller derby."

Devika walked into his bathroom to start getting ready for bed. When she emerged, Brad was sitting on the bed, fiddling with his phone. She crawled over the bed toward him to see.

"Who are you calling?" Devika asked.

"Megan. She's not answering."

"Um. Why are you calling her now?"

"Well—oh, she's calling me back. Hey, Megan."

By the way Brad was holding the phone, she could tell it was a video call, but she couldn't see the screen.

Do I peek? Maybe I should just let Brad handle this. Megan probably doesn't need to know we're sharing a bed, even if we haven't had sex…yet.

"Brad, what the hell? You know it's late, right?"

"Yeah, sorry. Megan, I wouldn't have called if it wasn't important."

"Fine." Devika heard the exasperation in Megan's tone. "Sorry I didn't pick up, but I don't think your yoga buddy would be happy if I gave you a free show." Devika covered her mouth to stifle her laugh. "Now that I have a shirt on, what's so important?"

"Speaking of my yoga buddy." Brad gestured Devika over.

He turned the phone so they were both on camera, and she saw Megan for the first time. Devika smacked Brad hard on the arm.

"What did you hit me for?"

"Brad, *you asshole.* You told me Megan was pretty—you didn't tell me she was smoking hot."

Megan grinned. "Smack him again, Devika. He certainly didn't tell me you were drop-dead gorgeous." Devika did as instructed.

"Ow!"

"Lemme see." Megan turned her phone and another woman appeared. "Oh, damn. Girl, smack Brad again."

"Ow! What was that for?"

The other woman said, "Because you probably deserve it. I gotta say, Brad, your taste in women is impeccable. I might have to steal this one, too. Ow!"

"You better not, Tasha," Megan scolded her.

Devika waved at them. "It's nice to meet you both and put faces to the names. Megan, I gotta say, you definitely traded up."

The three women laughed, and Brad whined, "I'm right here."

Megan added, "I'm starting to rethink stealing her from Brad."

"Not cool."

Devika leaned over and whispered in Brad's ear, "Don't worry. I love you, and I'll do my best to resist them." He seemed slightly mollified.

Brad forged onward. "Megan, I wanted to introduce you to Devika. Maybe we could actually meet in person sometime."

"It's lovely to meet you as well, Devika. Brad, why do you want us to meet?"

Brad took an audible breath before saying, "Because I want to make sure you approve before I introduce her to Sophia."

Megan's eyes narrowed. "Brad, you do realize you gave me veto power over your love life, right?"

Oh, shit. I never thought of that. Clearly, Brad didn't either. This could go very wrong, because I know he'll choose Sophia over me.

The mood was suddenly very tense, and Devika felt like there was a ball of ice in the pit of her stomach.

"Devika, do you want to meet our daughter?"

"Yes, Megan. Very much. She's important to Brad, so she's important to me."

"I like you so far, and you do seem to have a positive effect on my ex-husband. Let's meet, the four of us." Megan turned to Tasha, asking, "Are you good with meeting them?"

"Yeah. What about spring break? Sophia's in camp all day, and we can have Quincy look after her if need be."

"Good idea." Megan turned back to the phone. "Quincy is our friend. His daughter, Ruby, is Sophia's best friend. They skate together. They're practically sisters at this point."

Devika saw Brad give her a questioning look. She responded with a nod.

"Sure. We can come down during spring break."

"Perfect."

Devika felt the ball of ice in her stomach melting. "Megan," Devika said breezily. "Maybe we could do yoga while we're down there."

Megan and Tasha looked at each other and started giggling. Tasha said, "Oh, we definitely need to get her into the Wednesday class."

"What's the Wednesday class?"

Megan said, "I started teaching a yoga class on Wednesdays...nude yoga." She looked at Brad. "No boys allowed."

Devika gleefully clapped her hands together. "Oh, I'm so down." She touched Brad's arm. "It's okay, love. Maybe you can fix us dinner or something while we're in class."

Megan and Tasha's jaws dropped. Megan recovered first. "Since when does *Brad* cook?"

"Hey, I'm still right here."

"I've been teaching him. Brad actually made a pretty good *chana masala* last week. Didn't you, sweetie?"

Megan looked stunned. "*Holy. Shit.* I have so many questions right now."

Brad responded, "Maybe we could save those questions—and whatever scraps of my dignity remain—for another time. It's late."

"Bye, Devika. Good meeting you." Megan and Tasha blew air kisses at her.

"Lovely meeting you both." Devika returned the air kisses.

"Thanks for calling, Brad," Megan added.

"You're welcome. Goodnight to both of you."

He ended the call and sighed.

Devika put her arms around him and kissed him on the cheek. "Thank you for being a good sport. Would you feel better if I showed you my boobs?"

Brad tried to fake a silent pout, but Devika could see him breaking. She shuffled down the bed to be in his sightline. Devika grabbed the hem of her Green Day shirt and started slowly and sensually inching it up her stomach. She had his full attention as she slowly pulled her shirt up, keeping her hands firmly locked onto her breasts, lifting them as she went. Once at the point where she could go no further without letting them drop, Devika stopped.

"I mean. I don't have to. If you want to pout and not see my boobs, that's fine." Devika jiggled them seductively.

"Well, if you're only doing it to make me feel better, then it would be rude of me to decline."

"Okay, then." Devika gave them another jiggle, and then moved her shirt up, releasing her breasts, which dropped and bounced. She watched Brad's eyes follow their movement.

Once she finished pulling the shirt over her head, Devika casually tossed it aside and crawled back up the bed.

Mm. I feel like a sex goddess. He's just staring at me.

"Brad, you said we need to talk things over before we have sex, and I support you. Tonight, I'm wondering if it's okay with you if we just sleep topless. I want you to hold me and feel your skin against mine."

"I'd like that. Thank you, Devika."

Once Brad was finished getting ready for bed, he climbed in, and Devika happily settled against him.

It's just like our first night together, but now with less clothing. I should feel more vulnerable, but instead I feel safe and connected.

Chapter 34

Desire

U2

A month ago, Brad would have woken up with an aching spine, but now he was used to sleeping on his back. This morning found Devika with her head and arm still on his chest. He could feel a small patch of drool around his sternum.

Brad looked down at the waves of dark hair, lightly speckled with gray, spread across his body. He smiled as he listened to Devika's quiet snores.

I have about three minutes to enjoy this before our alarms go off. Having her leg draped across me isn't helping my morning wood situation, but I suppose intimate contact is inevitable now. I just don't want to go too fast. Given that we've been sleeping together for over a month and I just saw her boobs for the first time, we might have been going a bit slow. I'm not going to worry about it right now. I just want to enjoy being here with Devika.

He watched her sleep, dreading the intrusion of their alarms. Time inexorably moved on, and their alarms began blaring. Brad quickly shut his alarm off. Devika groaned and rolled over to shut hers off as well. He placed a hand gently on her bare back, and she cooed in response. Rolling back, Devika snuggled up against him.

"Good morning, love," Brad whispered.

Devika grunted in response. As she wiggled into a comfortable position, her hand touched the drool on his chest, and she bolted upright.

"Oh my gosh, I'm sorry I drooled on you in the night."

"It's all right," Brad chuckled. "I'm easy to clean."

Devika snuggled back down, sighing happily. "You feel good."

"So do you. Unfortunately, we do need to go to work."

"Ugh. You suck."

Brad could feel Devika breathing against him. He started idly caressing her back, and he noticed her breathing intensify. Devika returned the favor by gently caressing his chest and stomach, and inevitably, her hand drifted a bit further south.

"Oh. My...Brad, is this for me?"

"Um, technically it happens every morning; however, it might be somewhat more pronounced this morning because of you."

"How have I not noticed this before?"

"You usually roll over in the night, which gives me a chance to think about baseball or something to make it go away."

Now she's stroking me.

"Do you want my help making it go away?"

"Devika, I would love your help making it go away, but I don't think I'm ready yet."

She sounded disappointed when she said, "Sorry." Devika adjusted herself to rest her chin on his chest, looking at him. "Any chance you might be ready tonight? My period comes tomorrow."

"I don't know. Can we talk later?"

"Of course." Devika slithered up to kiss him. "What exactly do you want to talk about?"

"About our desires, our boundaries, our interests, and—if you're comfortable with it—our fantasies."

"That's a lot, but I'm good with it."

"Would it help to write things down during the day, and we can read each other's notes and talk about it? Honestly and without judging."

Devika nodded. "I like your idea."

"Wonderful. I do need to get ready for work, though."

"Ugh. Fine. I need another kiss first."

"You're a very demanding woman." Brad grinned as she kissed him again.

Later, on his bus ride into work, Brad felt something in his coat pocket. He reached in and his fingers discovered something lacy and damp. Brad surreptitiously pulled it out just enough to recognize the pink panties Devika had slept in. He stuffed them back in his pocket, wondering which was burning hotter, his imagination or his face.

Devika's gift tormented Brad all day long. He felt like a piece of her essence was with him all day long, and it was exhilarating. During his lunch break and slow periods, Brad wrote down what he wanted to tell her.

Maybe not what I want *to tell her, but what I* need *to tell her.*

When Brad got home, Devika was waiting for him, wearing a black cocktail dress.

"Hi, honey," Devika greeted him. She remained on the couch, absently petting Cricket.

"Hey, love. Do you usually wear a little black dress to work?"

"No, I'm wearing it for you." Devika held up a folded piece of paper. "Where did all this come from, Brad? This whole share-our-desires-and-fears thing?"

"Hang on." Brad put his coat and bag down. "By the way, slipping your panties into my pocket was cruel. They've tortured me all day."

"Aw. I thought you might like a reminder of me."

"Oh, I did. I liked it a *lot*."

Devika grinned wickedly as she continued to gently pet Cricket. Brad could hear faint little cat purrs. He sat down next to Devika and pulled off his shoes and socks.

"Okay, back to your question. As you know, during my divorce, I started reading and thinking about a ton of different things. I had gotten myself into a bad place, and I wasn't a good person. With some strong-arming from Tasha, I started to pull my head out of my ass, and I've continued this process." Brad gestured at the pile of books. "Within this self-reflection, I thought back on my sex life. Basically, I've let Little Brad do way too much of my thinking at times, which is a big part of why I'm divorced. More than thinking with my dick, I realized I never really communicated with, or cared about, whoever I was with. So long as I got off, that's what mattered. Anyway, this realization led me to rethink my approach to sex. I've read some books and even taken some online classes."

"Really? Online classes? Like what?"

"I took one on expressing yourself, and one on"—Brad paused and blushed—"cunnilingus."

"Wow. Did you learn anything?"

"A lot, actually. It's not something I've done a lot of before." Brad cleared his throat. "Anyway, that's where this idea comes from, particularly the desire expression class."

Devika looked thoughtful. After some consideration, she said, "All right. I like it. I've got mine." She waved her paper. "Do you have yours?"

Brad reached into his pocket. "Right here. Who starts?"

Devika handed over her paper. "Why don't you start?" She looked nervous.

"Thank you. Remember, I won't judge you. I may have questions, though."

She nodded.

Brad unfolded the paper and started reading.

Brad, I'm not really sure how to start this, but here goes. I like sex. I prefer vaginal, but I enjoy giving and receiving oral. Anal is good, too. Just not as good as the others. I'd like to try anal sometime while I use one of my toys. More than sex, I really like cuddling. Skin-to-skin bonding is amazing.

I don't like choking. I've seen that shit in porn and it does nothing for me. Also, I'm not going to piss on you, and I'll beat your ass if you try to piss on me. Sorry, I know I'm being judgy. I don't think I want to do threesomes or poly. It's fun for porn, but probably not real life. Also, I want to watch porn with you. I like massages, too. Giving and receiving. I want to try a couples massage sometime. I want to try nude yoga with you. I've been thinking about that constantly.

I want to take charge and be in control. And I want you to want me to take control and not be threatened by that. It might not make sense, but sometimes I want you to have all the power, but not in a threatening way. We should share control without getting into arguments. I want you thinking about me all the time.

Here's the hard part, because we haven't talked about this. I would like a baby. BUT, I don't want to try for a baby. If it happens, it happens, and if it doesn't, it doesn't. I don't want to stress out about making sure we do it at the perfect time. If you don't want a baby, then I can be okay with that. But if I'm going to have one, I want it to be ours. I hope I'm making sense.

Love,

Devika

"Wow. Thank you, Devika. I never even thought about the whole piss thing, but I agree with you. Um—"

"Maybe I should read yours, and then we can talk?"

"Good thinking." Brad handed over his paper.

Chapter 35
I Want You To Want Me
Cheap Trick

Devika took Brad's paper, unfolded it, and started to read.

My greatest desire is to avoid the mistakes of my past. After that, my greatest desire is to be more giving and selfless. I've always liked getting oral and never liked giving, and I want to change. I tried anal once, and it never really went anywhere because neither of us knew what we were doing. I'm curious, but I can live without. I really want to experiment with new positions.

I like to have my ears nibbled and sucked on. Spanking doesn't do much for me, but I'd do it for you. I'm not sure I want to do BDSM or the whole leather and latex thing, but I'd be willing to experiment if you're into it. Another thing I want to try is role-play. Maybe you could dress up as a professor or nurse. Just, no cuckolding role play. That hits too close to home on the mistakes I've made.

This thing you did with underwear is amazing. I'm writing this at lunch, and I'm hard as a rock. Please do more. I love your saris, *and I want to learn how to put them on you. I feel like that would be really sensual. And help take it off later.*

More than anything, I want to be near and to touch you. Feeling your skin on mine makes the world seem better. I want to explore every inch of you with my hands and lips.

"All right. Thank you. There's some exciting stuff in there, and I'm excited to teach you how to put on and take off a *sari*."

Brad smiled and nodded his head. "Well, we both like touching the other, so that's good. You mentioned toys..."

Devika took a deep breath. "We're still not judging, right?"

Brad nodded affirmatively. "Of course."

She extended her hand, and he took it. "Follow me." Devika led him to the guest room closet where she had stashed some of her bags. She knelt down and dug up the bag buried at the very back. Devika twirled the combination lock, opened it, and unzipped the bag.

"Wow. There's a lot."

"That sounds like judging." Devika deliberately put a dangerous edge in her voice.

Brad held his hands up in surrender. "Not judging. I'm actually impressed. I never knew there were so many shapes and sizes." He knelt down next to her and pointed at a small one. "What's that?"

"It's my clitoral vibrator."

"You mentioned using a toy during anal. Is it the clitoral one?"

"It would be good. It's also good if I'm blocked, and dick isn't getting me there. Perfect for travel, too."

"Compact. I get it. What about the metal thing?"

Devika grinned. "I'll have to demonstrate for you some time."

"Wow." Brad pointed at another small one. "This one?"

"That's a wearable vibrator."

He looked puzzled. "Like...in your underwear?"

I can't believe I'm having this conversation, but it's nice he's interested.

"No. It fits inside me and also outside. It stimulates me in two ways, and I have an app to control it."

"Really? That's so cool. Have you used it?"

He sounds like a kid in a Christmas movie.

"Yes. I sometimes wear it while working or hanging out with Manny and Nelson. I can give myself mini orgasms or just edge myself, and no one else knows." Devika grabbed Brad's hand. "There's something I didn't put on my paper."

"What?"

"Risky sex turns me on. Like at New Year's when we were above the party, looking down—I wanted so bad for you to bend me over and fuck me against the railing, knowing anyone could look up and see us. Well, provided Manny and Nelson weren't there, of course."

Brad's expression was a mixture of excited and puzzled. "So, you want to get caught?"

"No, I want to feel like we could get caught. Or someone might be spying on us." Devika stopped to think. "For example. Doing it in front of a crowd would just be awkward, but doing it in front of an open window where someone might be able to see makes me hot."

"Got it." Brad looked contemplative. "Okay, what's in this box here?"

"Those are my anal toys. I keep them separate for obvious reasons."

"There's just so many." Brad quickly added. "Still impressed, not judging. Although if I was judging, I would give your collection a nine point eight."

"What? Not a ten?"

"Nah, gotta make sure you keep working on it."

"Shush." Devika couldn't help but grin at him.

"You know, you don't have to hide your toys. Just don't let Cricket get to them."

"Yes. Cat teeth would be bad."

"Um. Devika?"

"Yes, Brad?"

"Could we try your wearable one some time?"

"As in, you want to control it?"

Brad blushed and nodded like a guilty schoolboy caught cheating on a test.

"We'll do that. Soon."

Very soon. I'm soaked just thinking of it.

Devika packed up the bag and handed it to Brad.

"Why are you giving it to me?"

"I want you to put it somewhere you think would be good for us to have easy access."

"Will do."

Devika followed him into his—*their*—bedroom and watched as he made space on the dresser for the bag. Once he was done, she opened the bag again and selected a vibrator. Devika could see his hungry eyes follow her as she sauntered to the bed and sat down, hiking up her dress and spreading her legs.

He's not hungry. He's fucking starving. I feel so open, defenseless, yet safe.

"Tell me what you like."

Brad licked his lips. "I love that you don't shave. It's so natural and wild. The little bit of pink peeking out is..." He groaned. Brad's expression changed to an impish grin. "I also see you don't have any underwear on."

Devika shrugged. "It's the strangest thing—I misplaced my panties today." She gave him her best sultry stare. "Perhaps you might want to try an appetizer before dinner."

"You mean..."

Devika turned the vibrator on and rubbed it along her labia. "I want you to put your cunnilingus class to good use, and I brought a friend"—she tapped the vibrator with a finger—"to help you out."

She gazed at Brad as he eagerly pulled his shirt off and knelt worshipfully in front of her. Devika took his hand and gave him control of the vibrator as he leaned in. Her head fell backward, and she moaned as Brad's tongue gently caressed her throbbing clitoris.

Devika brought her head up and looked into Brad's excited eyes as he brought his lips to bear on her overheated mons.

Damn, that is fucking sexy.

Brad's technique lacked experience, but he compensated with intense exuberance. Devika hinted he should use more of his head, neck, and shoulders to reduce tongue strain. His tongue slipped along her labia and circled her clit, coaxing moans of satisfaction from her throat. He sucked and nibbled her pleasure button as he swirled the vibrator inside her, enticing her to an orgasmic peak. She stroked his hair as she came down from her high, rewarding him with a smile.

Not the best, and he still has a lot to learn, but sadly, he's still in the top ten, probably top five, for oral orgasms I've received. On the plus side, with more practice, he'll have me cumming like a rocket soon.

"I'm sorry if—"

"Brad, did you have fun?"

"Yes. I just know I'm not well-practiced at oral."

"Well, let me tell you—I had a great time. Just relax. Don't worry about being good or great or perfect, just enjoy being with me."

"I will."

Devika pulled her dress down and made Brad put a shirt back on so he could run out and get them some Chinese takeout for dinner. She fed Cricket while he was out, and they settled down at the table to eat their dinner.

At some point, Devika noticed that Brad had stopped eating and was staring contemplatively at the wall. "What are you thinking?"

"I'm just thinking back to something you said, and what you wrote."

"Like what?"

"How you like risky sex, and wanting to have a baby but not trying. Is there a connection there?"

Damn. I was hoping he missed that.

"We're still not judging, right?"

"Of course."

"I scared myself during my post-divorce slut phase when I discovered just how much I was willing to risk. I didn't want to be a single mother, but something about gambling with pregnancy...it got under my skin. I started craving the risk. I didn't like the person I was becoming, so I stopped, and I've built up my toy collection to safely take care of my needs."

Devika looked at Brad with growing concern.

"Brad, say something."

"I can't say I've ever felt like you did, but I sort of think I felt the mirror image of what you describe when Megan and I were trying for Sophia. Like...there was no risk involved. Instead it was this clinical tedium of building up before peak fertility. The sex became a job for both of us. It still took over a year for her to get pregnant."

Devika asked quietly, "Is that why you cheated on her? Because sex was a job?"

"No." He shook his head sadly. "I cheated on her because I'm an asshole."

"Brad, look at me. Old Brad *was* an asshole. New Brad is different, right?"

"Right."

"Now, my question for you—how do you feel about a baby?"

"Not gonna lie, it's not an easy question. I don't really feel the need to have a second child; however, I'm not opposed to one, either. I worry about taking time away from Sophia, but I also know Megan is her primary caregiver. You put it in an interesting way. Like you're okay if it happens but also okay if it doesn't. Correct?"

"Yes."

"And the risk of it sounds like it could be a turn-on for you."

Devika silently nodded her head.

"Who knows, maybe we could incorporate my interest in role-play with your desire for risk."

"Oh, fuck. Brad, I *love* your idea," Devika moaned.

He beamed at her before his smile faded.

"Not to be a downer, but—I'm not sure I want to have a child out of wedlock, and I'm not sure we're ready for marriage."

Devika smiled warmly. "I know. But maybe someday."

Brad reached across to take her hand. "If I get married again, I can't imagine anyone I would want to marry more than you."

I like the sound of that.

Devika brought his hand up to her lips and kissed it softly.

Chapter 36

Blow My Fuse

Kix

Brad woke up Tuesday morning just before their alarms. Once again, Devika's head rested on his chest, one arm draped across him.

I don't think this one month trial move-in is going to work. I want to wake up like this every single day.

He gently scratched Devika's back, angling his fingers to get the maximum effect out of his trimmed fingernails. His hand moved in slow, lazy strokes, teasing the soft skin on her back. Devika stirred and groaned softly.

"Brad. What are you doing?"

"I thought this might be a nicer way for you to wake up than those screeching alarms. I can stop, though."

"Mmm. You can stop, but only so I can turn off my alarm. Then I need more back scratching."

Brad fumbled blindly for his own phone, unable to take his eyes off Devika as she rolled over to fiddle with her phone. They both managed to cancel their alarms, and then she rolled back and snuggled into his body. Devika purred as Brad resumed his feather-light back scratching. He enjoyed feeling her writhe under his touch, her body alternating between pressing against him and arching away.

"Fucking hell, Brad. I don't know why you decided to wake me like this, but it was the best fucking idea you've ever had." Devika moaned, followed by a whimper. "Holy shit. You could do this to me all day long, and it wouldn't be enough."

"I guess you enjoy it."

"Enjoy it? I just discovered that my entire back is an erogenous zone. I've had my back scratched before, but this...this is heavenly. I have to try this on you." Devika shuddered and giggled. "But not now. Oh...don't stop."

Brad continued dragging his fingernails lightly over her back in languid arcs. "Devika, I've been thinking."

"Oh...if it's more thoughts like this, then please, continue thinking."

He chuckled. "We should book a couple's massage."

"I like your way of thinking. I'll do you one better. We should do a couple's spa day. Have you ever had a mani-pedi?"

"Uh. No."

"You need to try it. Trust me."

"I do."

"Mmm, I like it when you say those words."

"I do?"

"Yeah, but not with the question mark sound at the end." Devika lifted her head, beaming at Brad. "Those two words in a declarative fashion—hearing them makes me tingle. Or maybe your hands make me tingle. Probably both." She pulled herself up to kiss him softly. Devika stopped kissing, but held her lips against his. "Me kissing you was not a signal to stop scratching me. Mmm, *good boy*." The kisses resumed.

Eventually, Devika levered herself up. "As much as I hate it, we need to go to work. Sorry about the morning breath."

"Sorry about mine as well. Worth it to kiss you though."

Devika grinned devilishly. "Yeah, it is. Thank you for this morning, and last night."

"You're welcome."

Brad let Devika take the first shower while he fed Cricket. The coffee machine had automatically made coffee, so he poured them each a mug. Brad carried Devika's mug into the bedroom, but didn't see her there. He knocked on the bathroom door, which was slightly ajar.

"Devika, would you like—"

The door swung open, revealing Devika pulling up her underwear. Startled, she jumped and spun away from Brad. "What the hell? Don't you knock?"

"I did. Sorry, I guess I knocked too hard and the door opened."

"Damn it. I told you my period starts today."

"Okay…" Brad had his eyes closed, coffee mug extended in a peace offering. "I don't get it. Please don't think I'm insulting you, but why does it matter?"

"I don't want you seeing me with my—you know—feminine products."

"Sorry, I didn't mean to upset you. Um. Can I ask why?"

"Because it's gross and unsexy."

Brad considered this before answering. "I dunno. It's a natural process and maybe it's gross, but whatever. What if I was curious and wanted to see?"

"Why would you want to see?"

"Because you're beautiful, and I want to get to know all of you."

Her voice sounded hard, yet brittle. Like iron again. "Really. You seriously want to see?"

Brad kept his voice soft. "Yes. I love all of you, Devika."

"Fine. Open your eyes. Weirdo."

He opened his eyes to see Devika smiling shyly at him. "I mean it. You're beautiful."

"Here's the deal, Brad. If I show you this, then this means I can send you to the store to buy me stuff with no arguments or objections."

Brad laughed. "I'm secure enough and I love you enough that I will happily buy you tampons in the super-jumbo bulk packaging. I'll do laps around the store carrying them in my arms for everyone to see. They will all know I am a kept man."

Devika shook her head. "You are such a dork sometimes. Also, I use pads, not tampons."

"What's the difference?"

"You sweet, innocent boy. Did Megan teach you nothing?"

"If she did, then I wasn't paying attention. I am now."

Devika pulled her underwear down, showing Brad the pad nestled inside. She explained the difference between the pad and a tampon. Devika pointed out the first spot of blood on the pad, indicating her period was starting.

"Thank you for sharing with me. Please don't feel like you need to hide anything from me."

Devika's face lit up with impish glee. "Does this mean I can use my toys in the bathtub?"

"Sure. You can use your toys anywhere you want. Honestly, I liked having a toy assist me last night, and I'd like to learn other ways to please you with them. Actually, I want you to use them without me, so long as you promise to at least think of me while you're using them."

"Brad, I'm liking this open and a bit kinky side of you. You're serious, right? Like, let's say you come home from work, and I'm on the couch, double stuffing myself with two vibrators, moaning and cumming like a freight train. You're cool with that?"

"Oh, *damn*. I can't think of a better way to come home. Have you ever used two at once?"

"Yeah..." Devika looked shy and a bit ashamed.

"You're so fucking sexy. Seriously, please do it."

"Holy shit. You're not lying." Devika looked straight at Brad's crotch. "You look like you could hammer nails with the thing in your pants."

"Yeah. Um, you wouldn't mind if I"—Brad felt his face turning bright pink—"took care of business in the shower?"

Devika looked into his eyes. "No, I don't mind at all. Feel free to take care of yourself any time you want, but today I have a better idea." She marched up to him and placed her hands on his chest, forcing him backwards until his legs bumped into the bed and he sat down with a heavy thud. Devika grasped his boxer briefs, pulling them down while positioning his hips at the edge of the bed. She knelt down to pull the underwear off.

From her kneeling position, Devika looked up and flashed Brad a feral grin. Her eyes never left his as she leaned forward, one hand on his thigh and the other gently holding his member. Brad could see the light dancing playfully in Devika's eyes as her lips parted and her tongue traced the tip of his cock.

"Sadly, I don't have time to make this last. I need a protein shake before I go to work. Can you give me one to fill my belly?"

Brad groaned in something akin to assent.

Devika captured him in the warm and welcoming confines of her mouth. She furiously worked her hand, lips, and tongue in an intricate dance on his cock while her other hand teased his thighs and balls. Brad was already primed beforehand and knew he wasn't going to last long. When Devika moved her free hand to cup his balls while her fingertips brushed his perineum, Brad's eyes rolled back, and he felt the pressure loosening inside his scrotum.

"Devika, I'm cumming."

Brad fully expected her to lean back, but instead she fixed her mouth on him as he let the orgasm overtake him. Devika's hand stroked him softly and she sucked gently, coaxing every last drop from him before releasing him and leaning back.

"You...you swallowed."

Devika stood up. "I told you I needed a protein shake."

Brad caught her hand as she turned toward the bathroom. He pulled her back into his arms and kissed her.

"*Wow*," Devika exclaimed. "I didn't expect you to kiss me."

"I'll be honest. That's the first time I've ever kissed someone after they, um—"

"Blew you."

"Yeah, exactly."

"Are you okay with the blow job?"

"I was surprised by it, but I would've said something if I was uncomfortable."

"Good. Thank you for letting me do that for you."

"Wow. I don't think I've ever been thanked by the person who gave me a blow job."

Devika shrugged. "We should be able to thank each other for the pleasure given or received."

"In that case, thank you for letting me eat you out last night."

"You're very welcome, yoga buddy."

"Oh, speaking of. Yoga tonight?"

"Definitely. Now go shower, my love." Devika gave Brad a spank of the ass to send him on his way.

Chapter 37
Slow Ride
Foghat

As soon as Brad closed the door behind them, Devika stripped off her sweaty shirt and bra. She sighed as she reached down to scoop up Cricket. Devika managed to get in a quick snuggle before the cat squirmed out of her grasp. She flinched as a shirt flew past her head to land on the couch. Turning around, Devika licked her lips and ran her hands up Brad's chest.

Damn, he makes me horny.

Brad took her hands off his chest. "Go clean up while I finish dinner and feed Cricket."

Devika pouted at him, but Brad was unmoved. Instead, he spun her around and gave her a quick spank on the butt to get her moving.

"Fine. But you better still be shirtless when I come back."

"Deal."

She wiped herself down with a warm, wet washcloth, opting for a full shower in the morning. Then she put in a new pad and looked in the mirror.

He says he wants the natural me. Let's test his resolve a bit.

Devika walked out to find Brad, still shirtless as promised, cooing to Cricket as he tried to keep the ravenous feline's head out of the bowl while he poured the food in it. She sat down on the couch, pulling her legs up in such a way to expose herself. Once Brad placed Cricket's bowl on the floor, he looked up at her. Devika watched his eyes roam down to her crotch, observing his reaction as he took in her panties with the wings of her pad folded around. Brad didn't flinch, instead smiling at her.

"You're testing me, aren't you?"

"A little."

"I still love all of you."

"You know you're buying me pads next time you're at the store, right?"

Brad gave her a devil-may-care grin. "I know. I already took a picture of what you use so I can get you the right thing."

"Damn it, Brad. You're no fun." Devika couldn't help but smile at him. "But I love how you're dealing with this. A lot of guys freak out."

"Yeah. There was a time in my life where I would have freaked out. Now, I'm good with it." He paused and waved a hand at her. "Speaking of being good with something—is topless dining going to be a thing, because I'm totally onboard."

"Oh, so you like my breasts bloated and sore?"

"Oof. I'm sorry. Can I help?"

Devika shook her head.

"I do really like your breasts, though."

"Just more when they're bloated."

"Honestly, I didn't notice. In general, they're a good size."

"What size do you like best?"

"Whatever size you're comfortable with."

"So, you don't wish I had bigger boobs?"

"Nope." Brad looked at her quizzically. "Do you?"

"Sometimes. Especially in high school."

"In high school, I thought the ideal boobs would look like a photo finish at a zeppelin race."

"*What?* Oh my god."

Brad chortled. "I've grown up a bit since then." He held his fingers in the air so they were almost touching. "A tiny little bit."

"Men." Devika snorted derisively.

"Dinner's ready."

After a nice meal of Brad's latest iteration of vegetarian chili on rice, they adjourned to the couch. Brad sat down and spread his legs, patting the space in between. "Sit here, my favorite back slut."

"*Your what?* Did you just call me your back slut?"

He flashed his impish grin. "You know you want more back scratchings."

Devika shrugged dramatically. "Fine. I guess after this morning, I kind of am a back slut." She sat down, and Brad immediately started tracing his fingernails across her skin. "Mmm. I'll do anything you want if you keep scratching me."

"Can we talk about sex?"

Uh oh.

"I guess I did say anything."

"Thank you. I think I've been pretty open about how my past history of letting Little Brad do my thinking has negatively impacted my life. I'm terrified of repeating my past mistakes, and I feel like we've taken things glacially slow. I want to say how much I appreciate your patience with me."

"To be fair, it's not all you. After my recent experience with he-who-shall-not-be-named, I wasn't ready to hop in bed with you." Devika tilted her head and quickly followed up by adding, "Okay, technically, I did hop in bed with you, but not for sex. I can't believe you let me share a bed with you for over a month and never once made a move on me."

"Oh, I wanted to," Brad growled. "Trust me. I really, really wanted to. My own issues kept me from doing anything, and I'm happy about our pause. We were both in fragile places, and I think rushing into sex could have ruined things. After the last twenty-four hours, I'm beginning to feel like maybe I'm ready."

"*Finally,*" Devika sighed. Realizing how she sounded, she quickly added, "I'm sorry. I shouldn't have said anything."

Brad chuckled as he kept scratching Devika's back.

"I guess you're ready. I'm sorry I dragged this out for so long."

"Don't be sorry, Brad." Devika twisted around to look at him over her shoulder. "You weren't ready, and that's okay. I'm just glad you might be ready now." She glanced at her crotch. "Although your timing sucks."

They both laughed. "I guess I'll just have to keep scratching your back, then. Although, I'd be okay with trying period sex."

"Yeah, sorry. I'm not. Something about leaking blood everywhere doesn't make me feel sexy and desirable. On the plus side, I should be pretty light by Sunday and completely safe."

"You mean?"

"Yes. I don't want anything between us for our first time."

"And afterward?" Brad asked softly.

The million dollar question. We already talked about this a bit, but it's time to lay it all on the line.

"After that, it's up to you. Brad, I've made a lot of dumb mistakes in my past and risked everything for nothing. This is different. *You* are different. I love you, and I am willing to open myself up to *anything* you are comfortable with. If you want to use condoms during my fertile time, then we will. If you want my ass and mouth during my fertile times, then we'll do that. If you want to play the pullout game, then I would *love* to play that game." Devika turned fully around to face Brad. "And if you want to fill my womb with cum and let nature decide, then we'll do that. I'm all in on us."

Brad looked a bit shell shocked. "I don't think I'm ready for the last option yet. I guess I do have a week to think about things. One question—I know we said we would try living together for a month before deciding whether to make it official. Are we still having this trial?"

"I think that ship has sailed. For my part, I'm done with the trial."

"Me too. The test lasted all of two days."

They laughed again.

"For Cricket's sake, I guess I'm moving in here."

"You don't—"

"I'm teasing you, you big oaf. Your place makes the most sense."

"Our place?"

"Mmm. Our place is better," Devika purred. "Kiss me, then let's switch positions. I want to try this slow scratching thing on you."

Brad kissed her greedily before getting up. Devika sat down behind him and wrapped her legs around Brad, resting her heels on his thighs.

All right. Let's do this. I have the advantage since I actually have nails. Devika gently placed her fingernails on Brad's back—his skin shivered. She began to stroke up and down, keeping her pace slow and her touch feather light. *Listen to him groan. The bass was so deep I think I felt it in my pussy. Holy shit, he is loving this. I've never heard a man make these noises before.*

"Who's *my* back slut?"

Brad moaned back, "Me. Definitely me. Oh...damn. I will do anything for you if you just promise to keep doing this."

"Anything?"

"*Anything,*" Brad groaned.

"Mmm, *good boy.*"

Cricket hopped up into Brad's lap, and the room was soon filled with the sound of both of them purring contentedly.

I can get used to this. Devika smiled to herself.

Chapter 38

Astronomy

Blue Öyster Cult

The following afternoon, Brad took a break toward the end of the day. He shut the door to his office and made a video call to Megan.

"Hi, Brad."

"Hey, Megan. Is this an okay time to talk?"

She looked a bit irritated. "Yeah. I can talk." Megan turned her head. "Sophia, come say hi to your dad."

Megan turned her phone so Brad could see his daughter. "Hi, Daddy!"

"Hi, sweetheart. How are you?"

"I'm great! This is my friend, Ruby." Sophia indicated the girl standing next to her.

"Nice to meet you, Ruby."

"Hi, Sophia's dad!"

Tasha appeared behind the two girls. "Hey, Brad. Okay, you two. Grab your gear and I'll drive you to practice."

"I gotta go, Daddy!"

"Okay. Have a good practice. I love you."

"I love you, too!" Sophia waved at him.

Megan turned the phone back to herself. "Sorry, it's our week to take them to practice."

"It's no problem. Thank you for putting her on. I like having a chance to see her, even for an instant."

Megan gave him an appraising look. "What's on your mind, Brad?"

"Are they gone?"

"Yeah, just left."

"I want to talk about coming down to Portland with Devika."

"You're serious about this?"

Brad tried not to sound exasperated. "Yes. Very serious. I want to introduce Devika to Sophia. I also want to be very clear about something—this isn't giving you veto power over my relationship. I love Devika, and nothing is going to change my feelings."

"So, if you're sure about her, why does she need to meet with me, then?"

"Partially, Devika really wants to meet you. So, I'm honoring her wish."

Megan nodded.

"Part of it is you."

"How so?"

"You told me Sophia needed a father in her life. Also, you could have taken me to the cleaners for all the shit I did to you, but you didn't. Despite everything, you gave me the chance to be a better person. I believe I'm making the best of the opportunity I've been given, and my relationship with Devika is part of my growth."

"What if I meet her and say no?"

"Then I'll accept your decision and be a part of Sophia's life to the best of my ability, but Devika is part of my life now. She's moving in with me."

"So it's getting serious."

"Megan, it already is serious. I can't imagine my life without her."

"Oh."

"Does that bother you?"

"A bit. I'm beyond happy with Tasha, but a little part of me can't help but think I should have been the one you couldn't imagine life without."

"I feel the same way. You are wonderful and amazing, and I should have been better to you, better to Sophia. I sometimes wish I could do it all over again, but then I see you with Tasha, and I realize I was standing in the way of the true love of your life. The two of you have a deeper love than the two of us ever had. In Devika, I know I've found the kind of love you have with Tasha."

Megan wiped away a tear. "Fuck off, Brad." She didn't sound angry—more wistful.

"Damn it, Megan. Don't cry, or I'm gonna cry."

"I'm happy for you and Devika. Have you talked about anything beyond moving in?"

He felt warm blood flush his neck and cheeks. "We talked about *not trying* to have a baby but letting Mother Nature decide."

"Oh. Wow. I was thinking more on the lines of marriage."

"Marriage. Right. We both want to be together, we just haven't defined what together looks like."

Megan shook her head. "I get that. I knew I wanted to spend my life with Tasha but didn't know if I wanted to get married, and then one day—I surprised us both and told her I wanted to marry her."

"How did you know?"

"I just did. It felt like I couldn't imagine anything else." Megan stared at him. "Brad, are you crying?"

"Allergies. It's allergies."

"Sure..."

"Okay. I'm better now."

"Uh-huh. Let's plan this out."

Chapter 39

You Shook Me All Night Long

AC/DC

Devika was greeted at the door by the smell of garlic. She walked in and immediately went to stand in the doorway to the kitchen. Brad was busy at the stove, singing along to *You Shook Me All Night Long* and stirring something. Devika leaned up against the doorframe and watched him work.

He's actually becoming a half-decent cook. I still wouldn't trust him with Indian food, but he can at least make most Italian basics. His ass looks good in those shorts, too. Damn, he's cute. Can't hold a tune to save his life, though.

Brad spun around to mime the guitar solo on his wooden spoon. His eyes were closed, and he had the classic White man's overbite going as he tried to follow Angus Young's chords. As the guitar solo ended, Devika joined his singing. Knowing she couldn't match Brian Johnson's raspy vocals, she opted for a more sultry approach. Brad's eyes popped open as he realized he wasn't alone. His cheeks flushed, but he gamely continued on, and they finished in a duet.

"Hi. How long were you watching me?"

"Long enough to remember why I fell in love with you."

"I love you, too. Shrimp scampi sound good for dinner?"

"Sounds perfect. Then yoga?"

"Yep. Why don't you put your stuff down, and I'll bring dinner out."

Devika took hold of Brad's chin and brought him in for a toe-curling kiss. She whirled and sauntered toward the doorway, looking back over her shoulder at him. Brad's eyes were glued to her as she pulled her shirt off. Devika flashed him, then skipped off, giggling.

When Brad brought dinner out, Devika met him at the table, clad only in panties. Seeing his look, she bit her lower lip and looked at him through her eyelashes. "Shrimp scampi can get so messy, and I don't want to get oil on my clothes."

"Very practical of you," Brad responded breathlessly.

"Why don't you put the food down, and I'll help you be practical, too."

Brad placed the scampi down with unseemly haste. As soon as he stood up, Devika attacked his buttons. In short order, he was down to his boxer briefs.

"There," she said. "Let's eat dinner before it gets cold."

They sat down and served themselves scampi and salad. Brad asked about her day, and Devika related all that had happened before reciprocating the question.

"My day was good. I talked to Megan."

Devika's ears perked up. "Uh-huh."

"Are you good with seeing her and Tasha the second Tuesday from today?"

"Yes, absolutely. I'll take the day off."

"Great."

Devika got serious. "Brad, what if she doesn't like me? What if she says no?"

Brad reached out to take her trembling hand. "First, I know she will love you and say yes. Second, even if she says no, then I'll still see Sophia by myself until she's an adult and can make her own decisions about you. The one thing that will not change—will *never* change—is how much I love you. I'm not letting you go, no matter what Megan says." Devika could hear the urgency in Brad's voice.

And the breath I've been holding for the past month and a half is gone. I didn't realize how much I feared this moment until right now. Brad loves me, and he's mine—and I'm his.

"Thank you, Brad. You have no idea what this means to me." Devika sighed contentedly. "I know Megan will like me, and she'll let Sophia meet me, but hearing you say you love me no matter what means everything to me." She squeezed Brad's hand happily.

"You're welcome, Devika."

The next few days passed uneventfully, outside of moving Devika's stuff in on Saturday with Manny and Nelson's help. They congratulated Devika and Brad on this momentous step and went out to a nice restaurant to celebrate. Manny and Nelson talked about their wedding plans. They wanted to be married in November, just in case the election meant the next president and the Supreme Court could decide they would no longer have the right to marry. That bit of planning chilled the atmosphere for a while. The mood picked up when Manny asked Devika to be his maid of honor, which she graciously accepted.

When Sunday morning dawned, Devika slid quietly out of bed. She checked her pantyliner, glad to see only a few spots. Removing her underwear, she walked back into the bedroom to find Brad staring at her hungrily.

"Brad. Are you ready?"

He nodded.

"I need to hear you say it."

"Devika, I'm ready for you."

She slid back into the bed and pulled the covers down. "It doesn't look like it. Here, let me help." Devika tugged at Brad's underwear, pulling them down and off. She looked him in the eyes and said, "How do you want me?"

Brad gazed back, and replied, "In control."

Devika moaned in gratitude. She hopped out of bed and went to the toybox, grabbing a few friends before returning to the bed. Leaning forward, she used one hand to stroke Brad's cock while her other hand stroked her clit and labia, spreading her natural wetness. Once she felt ready, Devika applied some lube to Brad and straddled him. Placing his tip at her entrance, she circled him around her soft walls. Devika observed triumphantly as Brad groaned and his eyes rolled back. He started to thrust upwards, but she used a hand to stop him.

"Oh no, Brad. You said I'm in control."

He whimpered as she teased his prick with her nether lips, but he stayed perfectly still. "*Good boy,*" Devika murmured.

Brad pleaded for mercy with his eyes. Devika watched as his yearning turned to ecstasy as she lowered herself down, slipping him inside. They moaned in unison when her clitoris reached his pelvis.

Devika leaned down to kiss Brad, slowly and passionately. She held the rest of herself still, savoring the feeling of fullness. When she stopped the kiss to suck in oxygen, Brad said tenderly, "I love you."

"I love you, too." Heartened by their mutual affection, Devika began to move in long and sensual motions. She made tender, deliberate love to Brad, relishing their connection. They kissed and stroked each other, purring words of affection and admiration. Eventually, the feeling overcame Brad, and Devika felt him erupt inside of her. She slowed to a halt, lying on top of him as his breathing subsided.

"Did you—"

"Shh. It doesn't matter. This wasn't about cumming. I wanted to connect with you physically and fully."

"I love you. Thank you, Devika. I do feel more connected to you."

"That's good. If you're okay with it, I want to stay like this for a while. Later on, I would like to cum. If someone isn't *up* for it, then I have a selection of toys to assist in the effort."

"I want to—no, I *need* to stay like this with you for as long as you want. When you're ready, I'll help get you off in whatever way works for you."

"Thank you, my love."

Chapter 40
High Enough
Damn Yankees

Just over a week later, Brad and Devika disembarked at Portland's Union Station, meeting Megan and Tasha in the station lobby. The four greeted each other with tentative hugs before heading to Powell's Books. Once there, they had another awkward moment as everyone looked at each other.

Brad suggested, "Maybe we should split up for a bit and meet back here in an hour?"

Megan responded, "I'm okay with splitting up, I guess. I'm heading to the romance section."

Tasha gave an exaggerated eye roll. "Ugh, I'm off to mysteries."

Devika chimed in, "I'm a romance girlie. Can I join you, Megan?"

"Sure. I would like the company."

Devika looked at Brad. "What about you, *mera pyar*?"

"History and social sciences, I guess."

Tasha asked Brad, "How many books have you read for fun in the past four months?"

"None."

"Come on, let's go to the mystery section. Science fiction is right next to it."

Megan watched Tasha and Brad depart. "I never thought I would see those two voluntarily do something together."

"They don't like each other?"

"It's complicated."

"They both love you."

"Like I said. Complicated." Megan looked Devika in the eyes. "Are you really a romance girlie, or are you trying to make nice with me?"

Devika didn't back down from the challenge. "Let's go over there, and I'll introduce you to my favorite books."

"All right. You're on. Speaking of romance, how are things with you and Brad?"

"You know this is weird, right? Talking with my boyfriend's ex-wife about our relationship."

Megan guffawed. "Trust me, I know."

"We're good. Great, actually. I'm sorry he was such a dick to you, because lurking underneath is an amazing person."

"I know. I saw glimpses of that. It's why I agreed to marry him in the first place. I don't know if I'll ever stop being angry with him."

"Do you still love him?"

Megan paused to consider this. "Not like I love Tasha, but part of me will always love him. Part of me will probably always be jealous of you."

Devika frowned. "I'm sorry."

Megan smiled at her. "Don't be. I've found the woman I love more than anything, except Sophia. The jealous part of me can go pound sand."

Devika nodded at her. "I understand. I have a bit of the same feeling about Manny, my ex-husband. I'm so glad he found Nelson, though. Manny asked me to be his maid of honor."

"Speaking of marriage, are you and Brad…"

"Probably at some point. I have a lot of issues with marriage, and Brad has been considerate about not pushing me. My parents hounded me about marriage and grandchildren for years. Then they arranged the marriage to Manny, which was a disaster. They've never forgiven me for divorcing him. If I marry a White guy—they might disown me."

"Brad is about as White as it gets." They both chuckled. Megan continued, "What about the grandchildren part? Brad said you were thinking about kids."

"Kid, singular. Only if it happens. I've left it up to Brad to determine how much, if it all, he wants to knock me up. So far, not so much. We're not trying to get me pregnant, but if it happens, then I'm okay with it. Only one, though. Then I get my tubes tied, or

Brad gets snipped." Devika added with a laugh, "Maybe both, just to be extra sure."

"What if Brad gets a vasectomy before you get pregnant?"

Devika leaned close. "I'd actually *really* like it if he did, so long as he doesn't tell me."

"You wouldn't want to know?" Megan looked confused.

"No. I can't believe I'm telling you this. The risk of pregnancy turns me on."

"I understand. When we were trying for Sophia, I just felt something extra—it was exciting—around ovulation. Brad hated the whole process. It stressed him out."

"He told me. So, instead of trying, we're just not trying."

"You're in this for the long haul?"

"For the rest of my life."

"And how do you feel about Brad already having a daughter?"

"I like it. I see how much he's trying to be part of her world, and how much he loves her. Sophia makes him happy, and I love anything that makes him happy."

"What if you do have a child with Brad?"

"Obviously, I will love my own child, but I fully expect Brad to love each one for who they are."

"When we talked that first time, you indicated a desire to come to our wedding, right?"

"Yes, of course. If you're okay with it."

Megan smiled. "Would you like to meet Sophia when I marry Tasha?"

"Really?" Devika beamed and wrapped Megan in a bear hug. "I would be honored. Thank you so much, Megan."

"You're welcome, Devika. I'm going to tell you what I told Brad. Don't fuck this up."

"I won't. I love him so much."

"Good." Megan indicated the vast selection of books. "All right. Show me your favorites."

"Obviously, I'm a huge Lavender LaFleur fan. I also enjoy..."

An hour later, the four met up again. Devika jumped into Brad's arms. "Brad, she said yes. I'm going to meet your daughter."

Chapter 41

Afterword

The two brides were beautiful. Megan wore a green dress while Tasha wore red. They were chatting with Tasha's parents. Tasha's brother, Dante, and his wife were conversing with another couple. Dante's two kids were playing some sort of made-up game with Sophia and another girl.

As he watched this scene, Brad couldn't help but feel a bit nostalgic about what he'd left behind. Life as a colossal screw-up had left him with plenty of regrets. But then he felt a hand in his, and he smiled.

"What are you thinking?" Devika asked.

"I'm glad life led me here, with you. I can never put into words how much I love you."

She squeezed his hand. "Thank you. I love you, too. If you're good, then maybe you can find a non-verbal way to express your love to me later."

Brad's breath caught in his throat. Devika laughed as his face turned bright red.

"Come on, lover boy. Let's go see your ex-wife get married." Devika led him forward.

Heads turned and conversations stilled.

"Daddy!" Sophia bounded over to give Brad a hug.

"Hello, sweetheart. There's someone I want you to meet. Sophia, this is my girlfriend, Devika."

As Brad introduced Devika, Megan glided over. She stepped close and gave Brad a friendly kiss on the cheek.

"It's good to see you, Brad." At Megan's words, conversation resumed again and tension drained from the air. "As for you, Devika, don't you know it's bad form to outshine a bride on her wedding day?"

Devika looked down at her red *sari*. "My apologies, Megan. It's an Indian thing. We think a bride needs some healthy competition." The two women smiled at each other before embracing. Devika continued, "Besides, I don't think it's possible to be more beautiful than you and Tasha."

Megan turned to her daughter. "Sophia, did you say hi to Miss Devika?"

"Yes, Mommy! She looks like a princess, too."

"Thank you, Sophia. And thank you, Megan. I can't tell you what this means to me." Devika looked at Brad, then back to Megan and Sophia. "What it means to us."

Acknowledgements

Thank you to my wife, Cecily, for all of her support. She's my first reader and editor. I couldn't do this without her.

To our cats: Lady Starlight, Merlin, and our dearly departed Francesca, you are part of every cat in all of my books. A purring cat makes everything better.

Steve Davala, thank you for encouraging me to start on this journey. Four books later, I am catching up to you!

Thank you to Francesca Varela for editing my book. Thank you for helping me grow as a writer. (All mistakes are mine)

To Katherine Morgan, owner of Grand Gesture Books. Thank you for creating a wonderful and welcoming space for romance lovers in Portland. You were so kind to host my first ever book event. You are amazing, and I appreciate you so much!

Of course, this journey is much easier with friends and companions. I want to lift up all of the amazing authors out there. Special thanks to Stacey and Loren for your lovely and hilarious support. Also to my local author groups and the writing sessions, events, and everything else. This community gives me so much hope.

Finally, thank you to the Rose City Rollers community for your support.

Chris Walters is a romance author living in Portland, Oregon with his wife and two cats. When not reading, writing, or working his day job, he is an announcer for the Rose City Rollers. He self-published his first novel, No One Like You in June, 2024.